The Flames of Justice

Janey Clarke

First published in 2025 by Blossom Spring Publishing
The Flames of Justice (Devil's Mountain Series)
Copyright © 2025 Janey Clarke
ISBN 978-1-0684329-0-3
E: admin@blossomspringpublishing.com
W: www.blossomspringpublishing.com

CHAPTER ONE

"Jesse James! It's Jesse James and his gang! I saw him. They're up on the high ridge overlooking the trail. I reckon they're riding down into Nowhere."

The driver of the wagon from Duloe town shouted at the top of his voice. His wagon careened and rolled from side to side. At breakneck speed, he raced it down the main street of the frontier town of Nowhere. "Everyone—take cover! Jesse James and his gang are on their way!"

A regular visitor to the scattered group of buildings and tented businesses that comprised the town of Nowhere, the covered wagon was not built for speed. The onlookers watched as it jerked from side to side, and could only pity those hardy travellers that were inside. Goods, people, mail, and parcels were brought in by this weekly wagon from the nearest town of Duloe.

"Rubbish!" Manuel, the general store's owner had run over to the hitching rail across the boardwalk in front of his store when he heard the shouts of the usually surly, taciturn driver. He was joined by Amy, a young girl, newly arrived out west with her father and brother to Broken Horseshoe Ranch, who helped in the store a few days a week. The sweating horses drew up, and the wagon came to a halt. The frightened driver kept looking behind him as if the legendary bank robber would spring up behind him. "Jesse James doesn't come this far south. He's robbing banks and trains around Missouri Way. You need glasses!"

"It was him! I've seen his picture in the newspapers and on the wanted posters." The driver clenched his fists and shouted at Manuel, furious at being doubted. "I tell you: he's on his way down into Nowhere." Jumping down from the wagon, the driver stood, his frightened face towards a small crowd gathered in front of the general store.

Amy, who had joined Manuel, stared at the driver, then looked up the main street. No threatening horse riders or gang of desperados followed the wagon. There was no sign of anybody. "What do you think, Josh? Could Jesse James be here?"

A tall, muscular, blond-haired man strode over to join her. His finger pushed the hat back off his face, the better to look at the agitated driver. He glanced down at his companion. Amy's face was screwed up in concentration, as if reading the man's face would prove that he was telling the truth. Her hands were in her skirt pockets. Amy had moved out West after the death of her mother and soon learned what was important for a young woman to carry on her person on the frontier. She was a small and pretty girl with sparkling eyes and waist-length brown hair, always in braids or tied back neatly in one bunch. Josh knew that in one pocket there would be her gun. The Colt, her favourite pistol, was always at hand. In the other pocket was a knife, ready to be whipped open if needed. And it had been needed—and saved them both from death—on one occasion.

"Sheriff! I'm telling you! I saw Jesse James and his gang. They were outside town. What are you going to do about it?"

Hearing all the noise, the sheriff had walked up to the wagon outside the general store. He watched as the two dishevelled passengers stiffly climbed out onto the road. Ignoring the driver, he walked up to them. "Excuse me, folks, is he telling the truth? Did ya see the Jesse James gang?"

Brushing down their clothes from the dust accumulated over the long journey, only one of them looked up at the sheriff: a large, plump man. He was breathless from the rough ride he had endured those last few miles into town. "Don't know, Sheriff, we were being jolted about as that crazy driver put speed on. Dust was flying everywhere, and we were hanging on for fear of being thrown outta the wagon."

His companion, thinking he had got the worst of the dust off, walked over to the sheriff. "There was a gang of riders up on the ridge, but I couldn't swear to who it was. Don't know who it was, and I don't care. I want my bag and to get to the hotel. I need a drink!"

Amy glanced up at Josh, and then Manuel. Both men were snorting with laughter. They understood the man's need for a drink. As Amy saw him plod across Main Street to the hotel, she sympathized with him: he was still covered in dust, and limping badly after the wild wagon ride to Nowhere.

"If Jesse James comes into town, someone please tell me. Until then, I'm goin back to my office." The tall, thin melancholy sheriff turned on his heel, his black coat tails flying as he did so. His black leather boots trod a path through the dusty road that wound past the collection of buildings called Nowhere. Those who watched him could hear him muttering and see him shake his head. "Jesse James! As if Jesse James could be around here. Jesse James indeed!"

Manuel returned to the store, and began carrying the goods and mail being unloaded from the wagon. Josh, who had been helping him get the deliveries ready for their morning round, followed him. The horses were

3

turned around to go up the hill for food and water in the livery stable. The crowd gradually dispersed, leaving only the driver standing there beside the last of the parcels and mail that had been unloaded on the boardwalk. Amy studied the man as he stood there alone, a rather foolish figure.

Aware of her watching him, he gave a curt nod towards her. "I'm not mistaken. That was Jesse James with those men. They laughed at me; everyone laughed at me. But I was right. You wait and see, Miss Amy. I was right. It *was* Jesse James!"

CHAPTER TWO

"As if Jesse James would come to Nowhere! Why would he? We've no bank for him to rob. No stagecoach coming into town to hold up. Hell, there are only three businesses in Nowhere that even have a cash box!" Manuel had scoffed at the driver before he stormed back into the general store.

"Who *is* this Jesse James? I haven't heard about him. Can someone tell me?" Josh asked, following the others into the store. Having lost his memory after a severe blow to his head, he found it difficult to explain how lacking he was in the background knowledge they all possessed. It embarrassed him, having to ask them. Taking pity on him, Amy told him about the notorious outlaw Jesse James, and how he was renowned for robbing banks and trains. "Some call him a Robin Hood because he usually steals from the rich and gives back to the poor. They say he asks to look at a man's hands. If he has calluses, Jesse won't rob him, calling him a hard-working man, having earned his money, and tells him to keep it."

Manuel looked up from the packages he was sorting from the wagon. "I've heard tell that he is stealing all that gold and money to put into a central fund for the Confederate army. Even though the war was lost some time ago, they say there is a conspiracy for the South to rise again and make itself completely independent. All his ill-gotten gains are supposed to be put into this fund."

"Oh no! We couldn't have another war, could we? Everyone, and everything, was affected by the Civil War. It's too horrible a thought that there should be another one. Why do they want it? There's no need for it now, surely? I can't believe it Manuel, no one would want to go through that horror again, would they?" Amy's distress was obvious on her face, and she stared at Manuel.

The store's Mexican owner, stood clutching a large sack of beans. His brow was furrowed and the normally cheerful face was drawn into a sombre expression. "I hope not. But some former plantation owners want to continue or return to their old style of living, complete with owning slaves."

"Sheriff! Where is the sheriff?" The shouts came from outside the store. A rider galloped into Main Street and yelled for the sheriff whilst looking about the township for him. His shouts for the sheriff grew louder as he rode past the general store.

"It's Miguel from Dry Creek Ranch!" Amy called out as she ran out onto the boardwalk, looking after the horse and rider as they rode up Main Street towards the sheriff's office. "What can be wrong? What's happened?" Holding her skirt in one hand, she jumped off the boardwalk and followed the rider running up Main Street after him.

"Miguel? Isn't he the foreman at Nancy's old ranch?" Manuel asked Josh as the two of them followed Amy up Main Street. Turning back, Manuel shouted to his wife, Eliza, "Can you look after the store whilst we find out what's wrong?"

Josh hid a smile. There was no way Eliza could refuse to stay in the store. After all, she had her newborn baby, Isabel, to care for. And Manuel was always at the front of any crowd, eager to see what was happening. Running the general store with his wife gave the man a chance to be in the middle of any and all the action going on in Nowhere. Manuel and Eliza had arrived shortly after their marriage, taking over the store that had been built by the previous owner. The first owner's wife had hated the store, hated the surrounding countryside, and hated Nowhere and everyone living in it. Eager to sell, the proprietor had dropped the price, and Manuel and Eliza had jumped at the chance of obtaining the store for a reasonable amount.

"What's all the shouting? Hey, Miguel, what's the matter with you? Why are you shouting for me?" The sheriff wandered out of his office, and stood with one hand on his gun and the other on his hip, glaring at the man who had been shouting all the way up the street.

"Bank robbers! That's what the matter is. They robbed our ranch last night! What you goin to do about it? Took all our best horses they did, left us broken-down old nags in exchange. Emptied all our stores and made off with every morsel of food. At gunpoint! We were robbed at gunpoint. They herded us all into the barn and left us there!" The words poured out from Miguel, almost as if he had been saving them up on the long ride into Nowhere.

The thin Mexican took off his hat and wiped his brow with the back of his hand. His dark hair was damp with perspiration, and his face ran with sweat. He leapt off the back of his horse and called to the boy at the livery stable, gesturing for him to take the animal, which looked as exhausted as its rider. He stomped along the boardwalk and stood in front of the tall sheriff. A small man, Miguel's exhaustion was plain—but so was his anger at his treatment by the bank robbers.

"Well, Sheriff? What you gonna do about it?"

CHAPTER THREE

"First thing I'm gonna do is brew up a pot of fresh coffee. Amy, you better join us, seeing as your stepmother is the owner of Dry Creek Ranch." To the open-mouthed astonishment of the exhausted rider, Sheriff Lance Grey walked back into the sheriff's office and could be heard getting his coffee ready.

Miguel ran up the steps, pushing the door wider as he barrelled his way through. His anger at the bank robbers now included the sheriff and his lack of enthusiasm for his distress. "But, Sheriff ..." the Mexican began. A large hand was raised in his face. The fierce look from the sheriff combined with his hand motion, was enough to silence him. Miguel seemed to shrivel; he closed his mouth and stood watching as the sheriff went through an elaborate procedure to get his coffee just right.

Josh and Amy had joined Miguel and stood behind him. Josh raised an eyebrow at Amy, she grinned back at him and shrugged her shoulders. Neither knew what to say or do. They had known the sheriff only a short time, but they knew there was no hurrying the man. They also knew that when he did act it was like a whirlwind.

The coffee brewed finally. "Here you are," said the Sheriff and handed each of them a tin mug. Amy looked down at the strong, bitter brew in the cup. She shuddered inwardly but raised it to her lips and took a sip. Josh, who had picked up the coffee-drinking habit from Luke, Amy's father, the owner of Broken Horseshoe Ranch, where Josh was staying, took a large gulp and swallowed it, enjoying the bitter taste.

Miguel held his cup in both hands and looked down at it. Then, his puzzled gaze went to the sheriff, who had sat down in his chair and stretched out his legs, and taken two hearty gulps of his coffee before giving a deep sigh of satisfaction.

"Now, Miguel, from the beginning. When did they arrive? What did they say? How do you know they were bank robbers?"

The quick-fire questions took Miguel by surprise. He gulped the coffee, choked on it, and, after coughing, began speaking.

"There were six of them. Four of them sat on their horses with guns levelled at us. The other two came onto the ranch and herded us all into the barn at gunpoint. They led all their horses onto the corral and left them there, then saddled up our fresh horses. After that, they went into the kitchen, took supplies and loaded them into our buggy. Everything was gone— everything edible and drinkable went into that buggy. Nothing was said to us the whole time. Then the leader came up to us and apologized."

Miguel took another drink, swallowed it, and looked at them. "He actually apologized for all our inconvenience, and then gave us some money and rode off."

Silence. Each one of them in the sheriff's office was trying hard to make sense of what Miguel had said. He and his family had been fortunate. None of them had been hurt and, although astonishing and unusual, they had been recompensed for the horses and goods taken.

"What was the payment in? Coins? Or gold?" Leaning forward, the sheriff barked out the question, taking them all by surprise. The sheriff leaned forward; his insistence on the actual coinage puzzled the others.

"It was a mixture. What do I do with the money?" Miguel was worried that he might have to hand the

9

money over to the sheriff. Some unscrupulous sheriffs would demand it, and probably pocket it all themselves.

"Keep it—share it between you and Nancy. She should be compensated for the horses and the buggy. You, of course, will need payment for the food and drink they stole."

Sheriff Grey rose to his feet and reached up to a wooden shelf. "Here are some wanted posters, Miguel. Look through them before we go back to the ranch. Josh, go to the livery stable and get my horse saddled and ready—and another one for Miguel. Amy, you go to the general store and tell them you and Josh will come with me to the Dry Creek Ranch, and then on to see Nancy at Broken Horseshoe Ranch."

Josh opened the door, about to run up to the livery stables. Amy was at his back when a shout from Miguel halted their progress. They rushed back into the sheriff's office.

"It's him! I found the leader. That's the man who came to our ranch and held us all up."

CHAPTER FOUR

Josh and Amy ran to the table to peer over Miguel's shoulder.

Looking over his other shoulder was the sheriff. "I reckon that wagon driver was telling the truth. Not one of us believed the guy—but that's Jesse James you picked out. So, we now have the most infamous bank robber of all time, riding free as a bird around Nowhere." Sheriff Grey shook his head and made as if to swear, but took another look at Amy and swallowed hard. He may be a tough man, handy with his gun, but he always respected a woman, and would never swear in front of one.

"I reckon I had better take a good look at Dry Creek Ranch. After that, I'll send a rider with the news to the town of Duloe. I didn't believe that bandit was around here; not sure I want to tell anyone else before I am sure about this. Could look a real fool if everyone's made a mistake, and this ain't Jesse James after all. If it *is* that bandit, that ain't something I can handle on my own. I reckon there'd be a few other people who want to see Jesse James if he is here in Nowhere." The sheriff pulled on his long black coat and reached for the black hat he always wore. After checking his gun, he reached for a rifle. As he did so, he glanced at Josh and Amy: "Get a move on, you two. Time is wasting!"

As they all vacated the office, Sheriff Grey turned and looked back at the building. "I hope I don't run into that Jesse James. Not a lot of good locking him and his men up in my cell—blacksmith still hasn't made the bars for the window!" Shaking his head, he took his habitual long strides up towards the livery stable. Miguel, with his shorter strides, was skipping alongside him to keep up.

"I'll run on ahead and get Bella ready with the buggy. Amy, you tell Manuel and Eliza what's happened, and where we're going. Manuel will have to apologize to the wagon driver. He was right, that driver *did* see Jesse James." Josh chuckled at the thought of how Manuel would be furious to be proved wrong, and even angrier at having to apologize.

Amy followed Josh. She walked along at a quick pace but was still giving herself time to think about this latest happening in Nowhere. To think it had even happened at Nancy's ranch!

Rushing into the store, Amy shouted out the news: "The driver was right! It *was* Jesse James, Manuel. You'll have to apologize to that driver."

Manuel, who had returned to the store before they entered the sheriff's office, had not heard the news of Miguel's recognition of Jesse James from the wanted poster. He was ready to disbelieve her, but when Amy explained the poster had shown the man to be Jesse James, who had robbed the Dry Creek Ranch, he had to admit he had been wrong.

"Now I have to tell that miserable old ... man," Manuel finished lamely. His wife's eye upon him made him think better of his choice of words.

Amy grinned at him. She knew the Mexican owner of the general store would have loved to stomp about, swearing and cursing at how wrong he'd been to laugh at the wagon driver.

"Those men, Amy!" Eliza jumped in alarm as she realized whom they had both served earlier. "Do you remember them? They took those goods and gave us so much money afterwards. I think they must have been members of the same gang."

"Eliza, I think you have got it right—they must have been part of the Jesse James gang. That money they left for the goods must have been stolen from banks," Amy replied.

Manuel looked at both women, a worried expression on his face. "Forget you ever saw them. That money is ours. Don't want anybody taking it from us and saying it's stolen goods. I think it is best if you say they never came into the store at all." Manuel looked at both of the women, fearful that they might lose the money. Both Amy and Eliza nodded their heads in agreement. There was no way they could be certain of who the men were. It was senseless worrying about it. They were long gone.

Bella drove out of Nowhere. Josh and Amy sat silently for some time; both were trying to absorb the recent events and make some sense of them.

"Could it be Jesse James? Surely not down here? I thought he always robbed banks and railroads up north?" Amy finally spoke, a concerned look on her face. "After we've been to Dry Creek Ranch, we must warn my father—and everyone at Broken Horseshoe Ranch. They need to be ready in case they get attacked." Her worry was obvious, and she kept repeating the need to warn her father and brother.

"What puzzles me …" Josh began speaking. He frowned, trying to put into words what he was thinking and feeling about this strange robbery. "Why did they strip the ranch of food and any provisions that were there? Why did they put them all in the buggy? I thought bandits attacked stagecoaches, banks, and trains, and then rode off to another part of the country to hide until they were no longer being pursued."

"Yes, Josh, I think you're right. What if they robbed

all those places up north but came down south to hide for some length of time in Devil's Mountain? Sheriff Grey didn't believe they were here. No one did. Jesse James has never been mentioned in connection with Duloe or this part of America, so wouldn't it make a great place for him to hide out?" Amy turned excitedly towards Josh. "He was pleasant and paid for all the goods at Dry Creek Ranch because he didn't want any fuss. But he didn't bargain on Miguel's excitable nature and how he would run immediately to Nowhere and tell the tale to the sheriff."

"Yes, that makes sense, Amy. Maybe Jesse James has come here to hide away from all the men who are after him. It's easy enough to get lost on Devil's Mountain. In fact, it's the ideal place for a gang of bank robbers to hide out." Josh looked round at Amy and said thoughtfully, "Jesse James may be hiding on Devil's Mountain."

CHAPTER FIVE

Following the dust kicked up by the horses of the sheriff and Miguel, Josh and Amy's buggy joined the trail leading to the Dry Creek Ranch. When Josh and Amy arrived, they found a huge commotion outside the homestead. Standing on the porch, surrounded by bags and her four children, was Miguel's wife. Rosita, the small Mexican woman, was shouting at her husband so loudly that neither noticed the buggy's arrival. The old covered wagon that was normally kept in the barn and rarely used had been drawn up outside the porch. The two eldest boys were busy transporting items and goods from a load on the porch into the wagon.

"What's happening, Sheriff? Why is the wagon being loaded?" Amy said as she jumped down from the buggy and walked up the steps to the porch.

"I'm keeping out of it. Amy, I suggest you do as well." The sheriff walked up to Amy, his face grave as he gestured back towards the couple, who were arguing furiously in Spanish. The children were rushing about, gathering items to be loaded. They were heedless of their parents' raised voices and raced past them.

Pausing for breath and hearing Amy's voice, Rosita— her black hair tousled and flying about as she waved her hands excitedly in the air— turned towards the girl. Noticing the buggy for the first time and its arrival with Josh and Amy, Rosita rushed towards the girl and grabbed both her arms. She shook Amy and began shouting at her in Spanish.

"English, please! Rosita, I can't understand you. What's the matter? Why are you packing up?" Amy asked, trying to edge away from the excitable woman, who continued to shout at her in Spanish.

Then Rosita began gesticulating and shouting at Amy again, this time in English: "I'm not staying here. That bandit gave us money—lots of money! We take it and go home. I don't like this place. I must be near my family. Now we have robbers coming and taking everything in the house that we had to eat. I can't stay here!" Her hands waving about as she almost shouted the words at Josh and Amy. When she finished speaking, she stared at the girl and clutched her arms tighter. Amy winced as the older woman's fingers bit into the soft flesh of her upper arms. The usual smiling face of Rosita was no more. Instead, a scared woman— shaking with fear—stood before Amy. Her hair was escaping from her usually neat black bun, her dress was crumpled, and her eyes were wild and frightened. "Amy, I can't stay here," she wailed.

Taking a deep breath, she continued speaking. "Miss Amy, I'm not like you or your brother. You come to this land and you ..." Some Spanish words followed: "I'm not like you. I want to live near my family. There's money, plenty of money, that man gave us. Plenty for Nancy, plenty for us. I want to go home."

The grip lessened on Amy's arms, and Amy could only stare speechless at the distraught woman in front of her. Understanding the Mexican woman's predicament, Amy flung her arms around her and gave her a big hug. "Yes, it's best you go home if you feel like that. It will be a better life for your children if you can find happiness with your family. Can we help you pack?"

Miguel came forward and stood in front of Amy, who stepped back fearful he might also grab her by the arms. "But the ranch? There's only Nat left and he can't look after the animals and everything else if I go now," Miguel said, the worry on his face apparent at the difficulty he now found himself in. "And Miss Nancy, I don't like to leave her like this. She has been so good to us. But Rosita feels we must go now." His worry about the ranch was warring with his urgent need to carry his wife and family back to their home town.

Josh stepped forward. "I'll stay here at the ranch with Nat. Don't worry, Miguel. The sheriff can go with Amy to warn them about the bandits at Broken Horseshoe Ranch and tell them about your departure. Nat and I will cope until Nancy sorts something out. Nancy will understand how Rosita is feeling, and understand her returning to her hometown and her family."

"Won't you wait until morning to travel?" Amy asked Miguel and Rosita.

Miguel shook his head. "The journey is straightforward, and it will be cooler for the young ones to travel at night. There will be a full moon tonight, which will make travelling easier. Come into the cabin and see the money the bandits gave us."

The homestead looked as if a whirlwind had hit it. There were belongings and clothes strewn everywhere The children were darting from one corner and out again, adding to the increasing load on the porch. On the table, the satchel lay closed. Miguel stood over it, then opened the flap and poured its contents out onto the table. Coins clattered as they landed, crashing into one another until there was a large pile of silver and gold coins.

Silence. Even the scampering children seemed to hold their breath as they tiptoed past the astounded adults, casting sidelong glances at the table, at the adults who were staring down at the money.

"Stolen. Stolen from some bank or stagecoach," the

sheriff pronounced, poking the pile with his long finger.

Miguel clasped his hands together in anxious entreaty and stared at the sheriff. Rosita, behind him, was holding her breath. "Nancy, Rosita and I can keep it, can't we? It was in payment for the horses, provisions, and buggy. We must have payment for those goods that belonged to us. It's too much money, of course, but they rode off after tossing the satchel to us. They left it for us. Surely, we can keep it, Sheriff? Can't we?"

CHAPTER SIX

The entire cabin waited in breathless silence, waiting for the sheriff to pronounce his views on who should have the money. Even the children tiptoed past, wide-eyed and silent. Josh knew some sheriffs would just claim the lot for themselves. But he realized that this man, Lance Grey, was fair and trying to do his best in the demanding job he'd undertaken. Or did his preaching side come into play when making decisions?

Again, that long finger poked the coins. "There is no way we can discover whether or not this is stolen money. Those robbers gave you too much money for the items they stole from you. That was their choice. Miguel, I reckon you can share it between you and Nancy."

Miguel put his arm around his wife, and they smiled at the sheriff, relief spreading over their faces. "That is so very good. We can go back to our town and find ourselves a ranch or a business for us and the family," Miguel muttered. "It's so good."

Still, the sheriff stared down at the money, his face thoughtful. "If you're travelling back to live in a Mexican town, it would be safer for you not to carry gold coins. It'd be difficult for you to exchange or buy anything with them, and I fear could put you at risk from even more bandits. Folk would be suspicious of you, carrying gold like this on you." The sheriff pushed the silver coins to one side. There was a considerable pile, far more than the gold coins that were left. "Rosita, do you have a bag or sack to place them in?" he asked her. Rosita put a sturdy leather bag on the table. The sheriff nodded his thanks and began putting the silver coins in it. "Are you agreeable, Miguel, with this? Does this recompense you?"

"Yes, Sheriff, you talk sense. Miss Amy, do you think Nancy will be content with her share? She has been good to us. I would not wish to cheat her." Miguel clutched the jingling bag of silver coins to his chest as he spoke to Amy.

"I think Nancy will be very pleased indeed with this bag of coins." Without realizing it, Amy had picked up the bag of gold coins, and she too was clutching them tightly to her chest, just as Miguel was with his silver coins.

"I think that is fairly distributed between you. Nancy has far fewer gold coins than Miguels's silver coins, but they are worth more," the sheriff said.

It took very little time for the Mexican family to pack up their belongings in the wagon. The children were already sleeping: the arrival of the bandits, and then the upheaval of their lives as their parents packed everything away, ready for their return to their home town, had exhausted them. Amy hugged the Mexican couple, one after the other, before they climbed onto the covered wagon. She had only known them a short time, but they had become friends.

Josh shook Miguel's hand. In the short time he had known the man, they had become, if not friends, at least pleasant acquaintances. With Nancy in charge, there had been no treating the staff as inferiors. So, the ranch group at Dry Creek became more of a family. Josh, to his surprise, had been welcomed, despite them not knowing who he was or where he'd come from. He and Nat stood on the porch to wave farewell to the Mexican family, and also to Amy and the sheriff, who were getting ready to ride to Broken Horseshoe Ranch. The gold coins were placed carefully in Amy's satchel, which, rather than having over her shoulder as usual, she had placed in front of her, her arm holding it tight in case it should slip and fall. A precious cargo to carry, Amy was making sure not one gold coin escaped from her care.

The two men watched as the horse and buggy rode off in one direction towards Broken Horseshoe Ranch, the wagon in another. The dust clouds they kicked up faded into nothingness before both men turned and walked back into the homestead.

"What are the chores we face doing before nightfall, Nat? I'm going to sort out a bed for myself tonight. Is any food left at all? I reckon I'm going to be hungry before we sleep tonight," Josh said, and began straightening the furniture into the semblance of how it was the last time he'd visited Dry Creek Ranch.

"I've some food. Bunking down in the small cabin, Bill my war buddy, and I have a store out there. Those robbers stripped the house of provisions but didn't reckon on us having some. I got enough left to make us a scratch meal. Most of all, Josh, I have some coffee!" He gave his wheezing laugh at the look of delight that spread over Josh's face.

"Coffee! Good man, I could do with a mug of coffee," Josh said.

That evening, after the horses had been tended to, and the animals shut away, both men returned to the cabin. Josh had lit the potbellied stove earlier, and now the coffeepot sat upon it. The smell of coffee and the heat from the stove on their return gave the cabin a homely feel, despite the absence of the family. Nat had prepared his scratch meal, and both men sat down to some beans, bacon, and biscuits. This was enjoyed with a second cup of coffee.

"You really lost your memory? Or have you just hidden your identity?" Nat asked as they cleared their plates, relishing every mouthful.

The two questions surprised Josh. He had been sitting relaxing, but this surprising interrogation from the man beside him made him jump. Josh stared at Nat, who continued speaking.

"I only ask because it's often best for many a man after the Civil War to forget who they were or where they came from. Best not to say which side you fought on. That way, you don't get into trouble. But if you really have lost your memory, it must be hard on you," Nat said.

Josh nodded. He understood what Nat was saying. Neither Nat nor Bill ever talked about their war experiences or of their life before the war.

"Yes, I can understand a man wanting to make a fresh start, losing the baggage of his past, and becoming a different person. But that's not me. I woke up in the desert with Amy's dog, Meg, licking my face, and Amy standing over me. That is my earliest memory. Everything else I now know I've had to learn the hard way."

"You remember nothing else, only from when Miss Amy found you?" Nat's voice was incredulous. It was obvious to Josh that Nat still had his doubts and was finding it hard to believe that anyone could lose their entire memory.

Josh gave a wry grimace and looked across the table at the man. "Nothing. Sometimes I get glimpses in my mind, sudden flashes, but they can soon disappear from me and leave nothing behind. It's worrying." Josh's voice tailed away. He wasn't sure of this man. How much should he tell him?

"I've heard about it, you know," was the cryptic remark from Nat.

"What have you heard?" Josh asked Nat.

CHAPTER SEVEN

"What have you heard about me?" Josh asked again.

"Someone from your past is sending killers after you. It was all the talk on the ranch, but *only* on our ranch. We know to keep Dry Creek Ranch—and Broken Horseshoe Ranch—business between ourselves," Nat said. "You're being stalked by someone who wants your death. You don't know who it is or why they want to kill you."

There was a brooding silence in the cabin before Josh spoke again: "It's difficult trying to understand why someone wants to kill you. What did I do in the past? Who was I? What sort of man was I?" Josh tried hard to keep the despair and frustration from his voice.

Silence came from the man across the table from him. Nat cleared his throat, hesitating before speaking again. "The wretched war made every man I know do things he regretted. He became a man he didn't like, and most are now running away from that past life. If there's something that you did in your past that was wicked or stupid, don't worry about it, Josh. I doubt there's another man living in the foothills of Devil's Mountain that hasn't got a deed he is ashamed of, or an action he regrets. The only difference is that we have no one out gunning for us."

Josh was stunned at these words from Nat. The ranch hand had never spoken much to anyone, only passing the time of day when forced to do so. This conversation had been a revelation, and Nat's words struck home. "Nat, thank you. What you say makes sense, and I shall think hard about what you have said. Thank you."

Nat pulled himself up from the chair and laboriously walked out of the door to the tiny hut he and Bill had made for themselves. The open door showed the man limping slowly. He said nothing more, just raising a hand in salute in reply to Josh's words. His leg had been lost in a battle and he coped well with a wooden substitute, but it grew painful for him after a long day and heavy work. Josh had eaten a meal that Nat had prepared. He could tell the older man was delighted to have his company because there was a brooding silence over the ranch. The exit of Miguel and his family had left an emptiness that he could see Nat was finding hard to cope with.

The older man shared a small cabin built for himself and Bill. Partly made of sods and misshapen and bleached timber found in the desert, it had been home to the two men. Because of its ramshackle appearance, the robbers had not felt it worth investigating. The men's food supplies had been left intact, and they were now helping feed Nat and Josh. Exhausted, Nat took himself off to sleep after the day's excitement. Josh had noticed that the man was limping and obviously in pain. His war wound slowed him down considerably, and he could tell that the old soldier had done far too much that day.

But Josh could not sleep. He wandered out to check on the horses and looked over the garden that Nancy was so proud of. There was very little water on the ranch, and it had been aptly named after the dry creek because the swollen rushing river after the monsoon rains dwindled in the heat of the summer months to become dry and dusty. The ranch relied on a couple of wells that had been dug, and the generosity of the Grangers allowing the passage of stock through to the Avon River during the driest periods.

After his wanderings, Josh returned to the porch. He went inside and brewed yet another pot of coffee for himself, thankful that Nat had hidden his supplies away, and that they had not been found by the James gang. There had been a biscuit left from Nat's meal, so Josh sat on the porch, sipped his coffee, and ate his dry biscuit. Moonlight's purple shadows stretched out across the dusty landscape. Tall cactus arms stretched out in grotesquely shaped shadows, and the jagged peaks of the mountains loomed, black and threatening, over the eerie landscape.

"Whoa! You scared me, Cat," Josh said as the large calico cat jumped on the bench beside him. "I reckon you're lonely. You must be missing the family because Rosita's kids made such a fuss of you. You're going to have to make do with me tonight." He stroked the cat, pleased to have the company as it rubbed against him, settled down and began purring loudly.

The biscuit finished, the coffee drunk, and still Josh remained sitting there. A cooling breeze wafted over his face and he sat back, enjoying it and looking up at the sky. A million stars above him looked like diamonds, and he marvelled at the sheer wonder of the expanse of sky above him.

Turning to the cat, he began speaking. "Josh Barnes— that was the name on a piece of paper Amy found on me. But I don't think Josh Barnes is my name." His voice pleased the calico cat that sat on the porch beside him, and it seemed to move closer to him, stretching out a paw on his knee. "D'you think Josh is my name? I don't." The cat's head tilted on one side, as if considering the question. "You, my pussycat friend, know everything that has happened to you. I don't. My life is a complete blank until I met Amy."

Sometime later, Josh stood and stretched, deciding it

was time to get some sleep. The jangled thoughts in his head could not be quieted, nor the questions answered that night. One thing he *had* resolved: he loved this land, and could not imagine ever leaving it. No matter what he found out about his past, who he was, or where he'd come from, none of it would matter. He'd found his home, and he would stay no matter what was in his past.

Nat had lit the lamp earlier and turned it down low on the table. Josh, entering the room, was pleased to have the light. He'd never been to Dry Creek Ranch before and was uncertain what accommodation the homestead had. The large room, which had the stove and provisions at one end, was obviously where Rosita had cooked the meals. A table with four chairs stood in the centre. Two large, comfortable chairs with padding sat near the stove. Josh reckoned that Nancy and her husband, when he was alive, had sat there in the evening, especially in the chilly winter nights. In their turn, Rosita and Miguel must have used them too.

The cat had followed him in and stood beneath a cupboard, staring at him. "I think you're asking for food," said Josh. He wasn't hungry: that had been a good meal Nat had cooked for them both, but he wandered over and found some leftover scraps suitable for the cat. He put them on a tin plate on the floor.

"You enjoyed those, didn't you? Now I have to find out where I'm going to sleep," said Josh. He was grateful for the cat's company. Ever since he'd been found unconscious in the desert by Amy, he'd never been alone. It was strange to find himself in this place, with surroundings that were new to him, and alone but for the company of the cat.

There were two doors on either side of the main room.

Opening one, he found a room containing a single bed, and lingering in the room was the faint smell of cheroots. He then walked across the main room and pushed open the other door. Shelves lined the walls. Large shelves. "I reckon those were beds for the children, and the big bed was for Miguel and Rosita." The cat had joined him and looked in the room but turned away and walked to the single bedroom before jumping on the end of the bed and licking himself.

There was the bed, a couple of blankets, and a sort of cushiony pillow. "Nancy must have taken all her bedding with her to Broken Horseshoe Ranch. Still, I can cope with this—a bed is better than sleeping on the floor, as I usually do at Broken Horseshoe Ranch."

Suddenly, the cat stopped licking its paw. Josh looked at the strange position it was in: head up, ears twitching, and that back paw stuck up in mid-air. An intent look had crossed the cat's face, and it stared at the door behind Josh.

"You've heard something, haven't you?" Josh whispered and slowly walked to the centre of the room, placing the lamp on the table. He eased his gun out of its holster and tiptoed to the door.

CHAPTER EIGHT

Amy felt strangely alone as she drove along in the buggy towards Broken Horseshoe Ranch. She had been so used to having Josh beside her that to be driving on her own towards the ranch didn't seem right. The sheriff had ridden alongside her for a short while, but gave her a nod and wave and rode off at a much faster speed than poor Bella could keep up with.

"Never mind, Bella, you just take your time. I'll let the sheriff tell the others about Jesse James and the gold." It was silly talking to the horse. But Amy felt the need to sort out her thoughts. This time alone, as she trundled along, gave her the ideal opportunity. What would Nancy do now? The ranch had been bought by her husband. Nancy had been taken aback when he announced they were moving from their settled life back east to come out and live in the wilds of the frontier country.

Nancy had explained it all to Amy during a moment when they were sitting alone on the porch at the end of a hot day. It had been when Nancy had been a quiet, dutiful wife who had followed all her husband's plans. "When we got out here, he hated it and wanted to move back east again. But then, he finally confessed to me—he'd lost all our savings with his gambling. Out here, there was no gambling, no going out to saloons, and the little money we had left would keep us going on Dry Creek Ranch. When we arrived, Nowhere—as a town— didn't exist. After we had been here about a year, a guy arrived and set up the general store. He said it was in the middle of *nowhere*. That remark stuck, and it was how the town got its name. There was only the livery stable, housed in the old adobe house with its lean-to, to begin with." Nancy paused in her story and took another sip of whiskey before continuing.

"My husband couldn't take to the life out here. He hated the open spaces, the heat, the insects, the snakes, and the overpowering mountains behind us. He began to curse Devil's Mountain and walked around the property, shaking his fist and shouting at it." Nancy had shaken her head at the memory, before continuing her story. "Dry Creek Ranch was aptly named; only in the monsoon rains do we ever get plenty of water. It wasn't until one day he broke down and admitted he hadn't bought the ranch at all—he'd lost everything: our house and the furniture in it. The guy who won everything from him took pity on him and signed over the deeds to Dry Creek Ranch, knowing it to be a dud."

Amy remembered these words she'd heard from Nancy. It was hard to reconcile the confident, abrupt woman who ran the Dry Creek Ranch—and dealt with everything this harsh environment and its unpredictable weather could throw at her—with a quiet, submissive wife.

"What did you do? What did you say to him?" Amy had asked Nancy these questions. The older woman had smiled at her. "I said nothing to him. Never again did I speak to him. It was impossible to control my anger and fury at how he had deceived me. Yet, he wanted my sympathy. After we began losing cattle and crops because of the drought, he went off one day and shot himself." Nancy had told Amy her story unemotionally, as if describing a routine occurrence.

Amy's sympathetic gasps of horror had made the older woman smile. "Don't feel sorry for me, Amy: it was the best thing that could have happened to me. There was an old boy on the ranch, and his knowledge of the area and the animals helped me survive. In the driest weather, the Grangers let me use a cattle trail down to the river on their land to water the stock. That first year was hard; the second became easier—or perhaps I grew tougher." Nancy had pulled out her cheroots and smoked one of them for a few moments before stubbing it out and putting it back in the packet. Her small idiosyncrasy was no longer surprising to the girl. It was just Nancy, and what one expected from this strong, forthright woman.

"I can't believe that you were a meek wife obeying your husband in all things." Amy shook her head. "It doesn't seem possible, knowing you as you are now."

"No Amy, it doesn't seem possible to me either. If I had married some other caring man with a steady job and a secure lifestyle, who knows? I might still have been a meek, dutiful wife." Nancy gave a sharp bark of laughter. "We'll never know, but I am who I am now. I warn you, Amy, this land changes you. It's done that already. You are no longer the girl you were when you first arrived out here, are you?"

Amy drove up to the hitching rail outside the homestead of Broken Horseshoe Ranch. The words that Nancy had spoken some nights before still lingered in her brain. Amy had known that life out here, when the whole family—comprising her young brother and ailing father—had relied on her, had forced her to change. Survival, that's what it was. The frontier did not suffer fools or weakness. To survive, you had to grow strong. A horrible thought struck Amy: was she turning into Nancy? Would she end up with tough, leathery skin, smoking a cheroot, and cursing as much as any of her men?

CHAPTER NINE

"I'll take Bella and see to her." Chan rushed out with Ben and Tom behind him. They all greeted Amy's arrival with beaming smiles.

"Isn't it amazing? Who would have believed it possible? Wait till I write this in my journal. Jesse James has come to Devil's Mountain." Ben's words made Amy smile. It was hard to dampen his spirits with the truth that the man had been called a killer. He could kill even here, in the foothills of Devil's Mountain. The man was not a hero, Amy thought, and disliked the fact that her brother and friends were thrilled at his coming to their locality.

The boys were so excited, and Amy felt she had to dampen their enthusiasm. "We're not sure that it is him. Remember, he's never been in this part of the country before. It could be a mistaken identity, just someone who looks like Jesse James," warned Amy. Her brother was so full of excitement; Amy could see that he was itching to write in his journal about this latest development at the ranch. He hoped it would make a successful article for him to sell to the newspaper. Certainly, this would be more interesting than the usual day-to-day routine on Broken Horseshoe Ranch, Amy thought, and couldn't help but smile at her brother's enthusiasm.

Ben followed her into the cabin, watching her as she greeted her father with a hug. The bag of coins was on the table in seconds. Amy was so glad to get rid of them. It had been such a responsibility carrying them by herself. There were only a few coins, but they were gold and could mean everything for their survival in the hard times that could appear out of the blue in this harsh environment.

The sheriff was sitting at the table, his long legs

stretched out in front of him, coffee in his hand. A man of few words, he'd said his piece on entering the cabin and now sat back enjoying his drink. Like Luke, the man drank coffee all day. A strong and stewed brew was exactly how they liked it.

The gold coins sat on the table, only a few, but so precious and unexpected. Each person in the room stared at them, wondering where they'd come from, and how they had come to be in the hands of the bandits. Tales of Jesse James had reached everyone, even those who lived way out of the towns and cities, where his exploits made headline news in the papers. Was he a Robin Hood? Did he steal from the rich to give to the poor? Did he steal for some other reason? That idea had been present in an article Ben had read out to them some time ago. There had been mention of a secret society, the Knights of the Golden Circle, whose aim was to help the South rise again and defeat the Northern states.

Nancy stood up and walked over to Amy. "Rosita was never happy at Dry Creek Ranch. She missed her family and, as each child appeared, she missed the companionship of her sisters and her mother. I think it's best she left to return home. The children will enjoy having playmates, but I wish she'd waited until I could get the ranch sorted out with helpers," Nancy said as she gave Amy a warm hug. "It's good of Josh to stay there with Nat. But it's my garden produce I'm worried about. Rosita and her boy looked after that for me. I'd hate to see it all go to waste, especially as Manuel relies on it for the general store. And we rely on the goods we get in exchange." Nancy shook her head and sat down at the table. She fingered the gold coins as if to check they were real.

"I'll go to Dry Creek. Chan does the garden here and

can cope with the cooking. Why don't I go over there and look after your garden for you, Miss Nancy?" Tom's voice came as a surprise as he, Chan, and Ben sat silently on a small bench under the window in the corner, watching and listening. "I think I could manage it for you, and cook for Josh and Nat."

"Yes, Tom, I think you could." Nancy looked at the boy, still small for his age.

But Tom had grown and filled out since he had arrived at Broken Horseshoe Ranch. Both he and his younger brother, Chan, had been sold by a Chinese uncle to an American after the death of their parents. Chan had arrived in Nowhere first, bought by an unscrupulous hotel owner, who, thinking he had bought a large Chinese man, was furious at the arrival of the small eleven-year-old boy. He had ill-treated him and, finally, when Chan seemed to have broken an arm, thrown him out onto the street. Amy had rushed in, bought the boy, and brought him to the ranch. Some months later, his older brother—Tom—had arrived. He'd been even thinner than Chan, also bruised and battered after a long journey. The death of his mining owner meant he was out of contract, and free to search for his younger brother. Welcomed by the Tanners, he had taken over the gardening and cooking at the ranch. His name, unpronounceable to Westerners, had been changed to Tom when he arrived at the mine.

"Tom, if you could step in for now, that would be a great help to me," Nancy said. She was staring intently at the gold coins on the table. "We need more tools and another buggy at Dry Creek Ranch. Do you agree we spend some of this money?" Her gaze went to Luke, who was standing by the potbellied stove, pouring out yet another cup of coffee for himself.

"Thank you for asking me, Nancy, my dear." His eyes twinkled as he looked at his new wife. Theirs had been a marriage of convenience. Nancy was eager to escape the clutches of a disreputable suitor, who was only interested in her property. Luke, with his worsening health, which had never fully recovered from the flu that claimed the life of his wife, Amy and Ben's mother, had agreed to the marriage. On the advice of a doctor, and chasing his dream of finding Jesuit gold, he had sold up in the eastern town and brought his children to the lonely ranch in the foothills of Devil's Mountain. Fearful that his death would leave them alone and unused to life in such desolate countryside, he had married Nancy, thankful to find someone who could take over the care of his children if he died.

"Will you stay the night, Sheriff?" Luke asked the man, who, although silent, dominated the room with his brooding black-clothed presence. "Both you and Amy must be hungry. We can give you a meal and a bed for the night."

The sheriff shook his head and drained his mug of coffee. He set the mug down on the table and rose to his feet. "I'm going to follow Miguel's example and travel through the night. It's a full moon and a cloudless night. Best I get back to Nowhere. Need to check Jesse James isn't up to mischief anywhere else. Remember now, be on your guard. Those at Dry Creek survived. The next ranch these bandits raid may not be so lucky!"

CHAPTER TEN

Josh crept over to stand behind the door. He lifted his gun, ready to fire as he pressed his ear close to the wood. Listening hard, he heard the faint shuffle of feet along the porch before they stopped outside the door.

"Miguel, Miguel—let me in. It's me: Sam." The voice, whispering through the darkness, reached Josh's ears. He knew that voice and, when the name Sam was whispered, he cautiously opened the door. Josh didn't lower his gun; he wouldn't take that chance. It was always best to be prepared for any eventuality. Peering through the crack in the doorway, he saw it was indeed Sam, and that he was alone. Josh opened the door wider. He glanced around behind the Apache and checked yet again that Sam was alone. Finally, he put the gun back in its holster and ushered the Apache inside.

For a moment, both men stared at each other. It was Sam who spoke first: "Where's Miguel?" he said as he staggered towards the chair.

"Sam, you're wounded. Let me see that!" Josh hurriedly went to his friend's side. Blood was oozing from beneath Sam's fingers as he slumped into the chair, his hand clasped over the wound.

Dishevelled, dusty, and unkempt, the Indian looked exhausted. He looked up, puzzled at seeing Josh at the homestead of Dry Creek Ranch.

"It's not too bad. I was lucky—the bullet grazed my side. Bleeding looks bad, but it's only a flesh wound." Sam lifted his buckskin shirt to see the wound.

"What happened? Your family, are they safe?" Josh asked, as he prepared a bowl of water and a cloth, bringing them to the table.

"Yes, they are safe. I left them in one of the old abandoned villages up high on a cliff. D'you know the ones I mean, Josh? They're scattered throughout the mountains. My family is safe there for the moment, but I shall need to bring them down soon. They've no food, water isn't readily available, and they have only a few supplies with them." He winced as Josh wiped the blood away, disclosing the ugly pathway of the bullet.

"Yes, you are right—you *were* lucky, Sam. It's only a nasty gash. What happened? Who did it?" Josh began talking, but Sam put up his hand to stop him.

"Where is Miguel? And the family?" Sam demanded that he be heard.

Josh finished wiping the blood away and looked at the wound, wondering what to do next. How he wished Nancy were here. She would know what to do. Taking a clean piece of cloth, Josh placed it carefully over the wound and looked up at Sam. "I think that should do it now. I don't know what else to do. The bleeding has stopped."

He walked over and placed the bowl of water on the shelf, ready to take out in the morning. Turning back to Sam, he explained. "Dry Creek Ranch was raided last night by Jesse James and his gang." Ignoring Sam's indrawn breath, Josh continued. "No one was hurt, but they stole all the horses, leaving their worn-out nags behind. All the provisions and the buggy went as well. But they left behind silver coins and gold coins before they left."

Whilst he had been talking, Josh poured out two tin cups of coffee. It was still hot, as the stove hadn't quite died down. He pushed one across the table to Sam before lifting the other to his lips. He took a swallow and then continued the story. "That was the last straw for Rosita. She refused to stay another night here, so they took the old covered wagon that was in the barn, packed everything up, and left only a few hours ago."

Gratefully, Sam swallowed his coffee. He looked up at Josh. "Rosita has never been happy here. I should imagine this was all that was needed to send her back home to her family and the town where she was born."

"That's what's happened here, but what happened to you?" Josh took Sam's empty mug and offered him another coffee.

"Yes, please—if there's any coffee left, I'll have it. It's a renegade Apache group. A few are wandering around, and they are restless and angry at the way they are being hounded out of their ancestral lands. They wanted my horse, so chased me and shot me. I played dead, and they rode on after my horse when it bolted." He took the cup from Josh, nodded his thanks, and took another large drink.

Sam took a deep breath and continued speaking. He winced as the pain in his side reacted to his movements. "I was coming here to see Miguel. After the rains, the creek becomes full of water again. There is a small canyon near the foothills at the very edge of the ranch where Miguel has always let my family live after the rains. He never told Nancy. He wasn't sure she would agree to it. Her husband refused point-blank the first time I asked, so we never mentioned it to Nancy."

"Nancy would agree," Josh said. "There's no doubt about it. What will you do now? Go back up and bring your family down to the Dry Creek Ranch?"

"The last time I did it, I was working at the livery stable. I don't feel happy going back into Nowhere at the moment. If I come back here, I'm uncertain of how to get money to feed my family."

Josh placed some leftovers he had not given to the cat on the table in front of Sam: "That's all that's in the cupboard. The bandits didn't bother looking for food in Nat's cabin. Do you know, Sam, I think Nancy would be pleased if you could stay and work on the ranch."

Sam, his mouth full of bacon, looked up, his eyes brightening at Josh's words.

Josh continued speaking, explaining the new situation that Nancy was now facing since Miguel and Rosita had gone back to their hometown. "Miguel had two young sons who helped on the ranch and the garden. Nancy has got Bill now working over at the Broken Horseshoe Ranch. There is only Nat working here, and you know how difficult it is for him to do a full day's work with that one leg of his. If you work here, I'm certain that Nancy would only be too pleased to let you stay on the ranch. Especially if you and your family help harvest her vegetables. They're all ripening now and are ready to sell to the general store. Both Nancy and Manuel would hate to see them go to waste." Josh drained the last of his coffee. It had been a long speech for him.

"That sounds as if it could be an answer for Nancy and myself. Thank you, Josh." With that remark, Sam stood up, shrugged his shirt back down over the wound and grimacing at the dried bloodstain, and placed his cup and plate beside the bowl of bloody water. "Josh, you're sure of this? You think Nancy will agree to it?"

"Yes, Nancy likes you and your family. More to the point, Nancy is hard-headed and extremely businesslike. If you can save her crop and earn money for her and the ranch, I guarantee you will be most welcome!" Josh said with a grin. He got up as Sam rose to his feet.

"Take one of those nags the bandits left. It will speed you on your way. They're better than nothing," Josh said as Sam walked out of the door. "I'd ask you to remain overnight, but I know you won't."

Sam shook his head and smiled at Josh as he opened the door. "Thanks, Josh, for everything." These words, whispered into the night air, drifted back towards Josh as he heard the footsteps drift away into the darkness.

CHAPTER ELEVEN

That morning, Nat arrived early with his fixings for breakfast (as he called the goods he brought from his cabin) to the homestead. He looked brighter, in Josh's eyes—and there was a definite lift to his spirits as he wandered in with the ingredients for their breakfast.

"Did you hear my visitor last night?" Josh asked as Nat lifted the skillet, ready to fry some bacon.

Nat's bushy eyebrows raised; he looked at Josh. "A visitor here last night? I heard nothing after the upheaval of the last few days; afraid I slept deeply last night. Who was it?"

"Sam, the Apache who used to work at the livery stable. He had his horse shot out from under him by some renegade Apache. They thought he was dead and left him lying there whilst they chased after his horse. He arrived here looking for Miguel."

"Where is he? Was he badly injured?" Nat's concern was obvious. Josh realized that Nat also knew Sam and thought well of him.

"It was a bullet that hit him in the side. He bled a little, but it was only a graze, and he was determined to go back to his family. Renegade Apache are wandering around the mountains, and those bank robbers are out there too. It's not safe for his family up in those ruined mountain villages. There's also the difficulty of them getting food and water."

"They could come here. We could use the help, couldn't we?" Nat's enthusiasm made Josh laugh.

Josh replied, "That's exactly what I said—I told him Nancy would jump at the chance to have someone like him and his family living here, looking after the animals and the garden produce." Josh sat down at the table and looked at the plateful of beans, bacon, and biscuits that Nat had whipped up in a matter of minutes. Through a mouthful of beans, Josh said, "I volunteered you for all the cooking. Hope you don't mind that."

Nat had sat down at the table opposite him and had lifted his knife and fork to start his meal. His hands paused at this remark. At Josh's words, a grin stretched over his face from side to side. "That I would enjoy, Josh. It's easier for me to work in the kitchen. I can't dodge out of the way quick enough to avoid some of those animals, and their unexpected kicks. That would work well." He chomped on a bit of bacon. "Miss Nancy will approve of that, I'm sure of it."

They didn't have long to wait to see if Nancy approved. They had just finished their breakfast when they heard shouting approaching the homestead. Both men rushed out and were astonished to see the Broken Horseshoe Ranch buggy with Amy and Nancy. Alongside the buggy were Tom, the older brother of Chan, and Ezra, the elderly man who along with his wife Leah had been living on Broken Horseshoe Ranch when Luke Tanner, Amy his daughter and son Ben had arrived. They were riding on Star and Bella, both waving hats and shouting at them.

There was the usual dismounting conversation between them, flowing in garbled bits. Nancy, of course, drew them all to order, telling them all to be quiet while she went inside and had some coffee. She needed it immediately!

The discussion about the fact that Miguel, Rosita, and the children were no longer at Dry Creek Ranch was the first thing that had to be talked over. Nancy was worried about the ripening produce and the running of her ranch.

"Rosita wouldn't hear of staying another night. They left yesterday evening. The sheriff had given them the silver coins, and they went off travelling by the light of the moon, hoping to reach their hometown by mid-morning," said Josh.

"Yes, the sheriff and Amy told us that. What I have to worry about now is who is going to look after my ranch and my garden." Nancy swallowed a cup of coffee and walked over to the stove for another one, then said, "I'm off out to look at the produce we've got ready to sell in Manuel's general store."

Josh had been trying to tell her all about Sam's nocturnal visit. But, as usual with Nancy, there was little one could do to interrupt her when in full flow. He followed her out into the garden and, as they walked up and down inspecting the ripening vegetables and fruit, he finally got a chance to speak about Sam.

"Sam appeared last night." Nancy looked at him in silence; she listened as he told her of Sam's visit and his proposal. "I hope you agree with me that Nat finds the animals too difficult to cope with. He enjoys cooking the meals, and I thought he could be your cook and delivery man to Nowhere. Manuel would help get boxes down, and Sam could help load them here at the ranch. What do you say, Nancy? Did I do the right thing for you and the Dry Creek Ranch?"

Nancy thought over the proposal for a moment. Then she gave Josh an almighty thump on the back. "Well done. That sorts everything out. I can return with Tom and Ezra, leaving Sam and Nat here, along with Sam's younger brother. They should manage fine, as the productive season of my garden will draw to a close in the next few months. If they need extra help, they can always get Tom or Ezra back again. Good thinking, Josh."

They began walking back to the homestead; Josh was surprised to see Amy loading up his horse, Star, and her horse, Bella, ready for travelling.

Nancy looked at him and grabbed him by the arm. "Wait a minute, Josh. I'd better tell you what's happened. Luke has been working through all the information he has about this treasure of Jesuit gold. The man has been poring over maps and books day and night. Now he has a new idea—he thinks he's been looking at everything all wrong. Nothing will do, but you and Amy have to travel to Lonesome Creek and follow these new instructions."

Nancy let go of Josh's arm, but not before she gave it a shake. "I don't like this obsession of his, and I don't like the way he's always dragged Amy into it. The mountains, at the moment, seem to have so many villainous types wandering about. Thankfully, you both are going away from the mountains and along the edge of them into the foothills. None of the robbers will go that way—they will go up towards Bandits' Butte. I don't think the Apache frequent the area of Lonesome Creek. But Luke wants you to go now. And take enough for overnight camping."

"Now? Luke wants us to leave immediately, and what? Spend some time up there?" Josh stood still, flicking back his blond hair from his eyes. He stared down at Nancy's earnest face..

"Yes, he wants you to go as soon as possible. Josh, take care of Amy, won't you? And yourself?"

To Josh's surprise, he caught the sheen of tears in Nancy's eyes. He gave her shoulder a reassuring pat and said, "Don't worry, Nancy. I'll take care of Amy."

Little did he know— it was Amy who would take care of him!

CHAPTER TWELVE

Both horses were laden, far more than was usual. Extra provisions to last them a couple of days were included with their bedrolls. There was no need to carry full canteens of water, because there had been heavy rain the last couple of days, and even the dry creek itself was full and almost overflowing. Their journey should pass along the canyon known as Lonesome Creek. Set in the foothills of Devil's Mountains, it was not the usual barren desert type of landscape around Devil's Mountain itself. This part of the region had more abundant water, with more streams, and the vegetation thrived, lending an unusual bounty to the wildlife. The Green Canyon was an unexpected part of the foothills of Devil's Mountains.

"We must hurry, Josh. It would be good to reach the canyon and the spot where we had halted before. There was a pleasant flat spot, if you remember, where we could be hidden from any chance passersby," Amy said as they rode along in the increasing heat of the day.

"I wonder if that's near where Sam and his family were hiding. Those cave dwellings we saw opposite were high above that spot, and Sam said his family were hiding out in some ancient ruined village. I know there are plenty of them scattered through the mountains. They provide ideal hiding places with wonderful viewpoints across the canyons and valleys. That could be where Sam hid his family."

They rode in silence for some time. Both were eager to reach their destination, but mindful of their horses' well-being, they did not push them too hard.

"Is it true what Nancy told me about your father? He really is improving?" Josh asked Amy.

"Yes, it's hard to believe how much better he is. He swears it was the medicine Sam gave him, that old Apache recipe Sam had made up specially for my father. That's how he's become so busy and involved in his research into the Jesuit gold treasure. I'm pleased to see him so much better, of course, but I wish he wouldn't send us off on these journeys into the mountains."

By this time, they were approaching the entrance to the canyon. Josh had never heard Amy complain about her father, nor show any disinclination to set off on these trips searching for old. He looked hard at her and could see she was looking tired. Then he remembered: baby David was staying at Broken Horseshoe Ranch. The youngster, Sam's nephew, was lively—and his energy was wearing to all who looked after him. Somehow, he had formed a close attachment to Amy, perhaps because she was the one who carried him home to the ranch after the murder of his parents. He followed her around, now crawling, and constantly sought her company. Of course, Amy had become attached to the boy and loved being with him. Amy left David when they went to work in the general store and, whilst the baby was used to these daily absences, he disliked it when she was absent for longer. But these treasure-hunting expeditions were far longer (and seemed to be pointless), and he could tell she was missing the child.

They dismounted, leading the horses down to the swollen creek. "We've to be careful, Josh. There could easily be exceptionally high levels of water and even flash floods," warned Amy.

"I'll never forget that flash flood we nearly got caught in." Josh shuddered at the memory. Amy had rushed him and the horses up the side of a narrow canyon. The steep cliffs were difficult to climb with the nervous horses, but they'd reached a ledge and safety. Amy and Josh had watched as the water rose along the canyon beneath them. Those roaring waters rushing along below them had been awe-inspiring and frightening. They could see, churning over and over again in the narrow canyon, the debris of fallen trees and tumbling rocks carried along in the swirling water. It had only been Amy's knowledge and forethought that had them climbing up the canyon walls to safety, and out of the reach of the water.

Amy looked across at Josh and smiled. She also remembered: "Yes, it's not something I want to experience again."

When they felt the horses had been rested enough, they continued alongside the bubbling waters that flowed over and around the many rocks that littered the floor of the canyon. The undergrowth along here was surprisingly lush, but the straggly, spiky branches seemed to grab at them and the horses.

It was getting gloomier as it approached twilight made even darker because of the high walls of the canyon. Josh noticed Amy glancing anxiously up at the sky, knowing she was determined to reach the safety of their previous halt. "Will we get there before dark?" His voice made her jump, so deep in thought she'd been.

"I don't know. I don't think it's much further, do you?" Amy replied.

Josh opened his mouth to answer, but she turned round to face him and put a finger to her lips. Amy pointed in front of her, then cupped her hand around her ear. Silently, they both stood still, their horses even sensing the need for quiet, for they didn't shake themselves or snort.

Then Josh heard it. A repetitive noise, accompanied by muttered curses. Amy slid off her horse and began creeping forward behind the cover of ushes.

CHAPTER THIRTEEN

A man was leaning over a large boulder. He was attacking it with a pointed rock and attempting to carve a sign. It was hard work, judging by the swearing that came from him. He gave a sigh, stood up properly, and kicked the offending rock. Slipping a piece of paper into a pocket, he picked up his bag and walked towards a horse that had been standing grazing beside him. He was wearing a greasy jacket over ancient Confederate trousers, and his pistol was slung at his belt, ready for action. The hat he pulled up onto his head was old and worn, and the grease around the hatband matched that of his jacket.

Josh and Amy waited for a moment, listening hard until the sound of the man's horse hooves faded away into the distance. Then, with a look at Amy, Josh rose from his crouched position behind the bushes. Amy joined him as they walked towards the rock. There was still enough light to see the images that had been crudely carved into the rock.

"Is that a heart? What's that beside it? Do you think that's a serpent, or is it a snake?" Amy asked Josh.

"No wonder that guy was swearing—this rock looks hard. He's not done a good job of it. But I guess that if you're looking for a sign, this would certainly do. Why is this guy carving out signs? Does it mean that he's going to bury some treasure?" Josh looked at the carving and shrugged. "Let's get the horses and ourselves settled for the night, and we can worry about what this means later. It's getting dark."

Amy gave a last look at the carving on the rock and followed Josh back to the horses. "Later—we'll think about it later," she agreed.

There was barely enough light left to sort the horses out and establish themselves on the tiny plateau of rock above the creek. Enough grass grew amongst the rocks for the horses, where they tethered them, after they and the horses, all drank from the fast-flowing creek. The bed rolls were placed, with their guns handy beside them. They both looked around to make sure they were safely hidden away from prying eyes.

"Dare we light a fire? Or would that give our position away?" Josh said, his need for coffee growing the more he thought about it. Amy stared at him and then peered down at the creek flowing through the canyon beneath them, and the many boulders strewn along the canyon floor.

"Up here, we are above any sort of trail. We could risk it—or at least have a small enough fire to give us hot food and drink. It's going to be a long night, and it'll be cold. We'll need a hot drink," Amy said.

Josh willingly got a fire going, and set about making coffee at a great speed. Amy had cast a glance towards him, laughing as she did so. "You know, Josh, you're now as bad as my father, with your love for coffee."

"I know. It's getting bad. But then I look at the sheriff and realize I'm not as bad as him," said Josh.

"I don't think anyone could be as bad as the sheriff. I've seen no one drink so much coffee, so bitter and black. Do you want any food with your coffee?" Amy teased him, as she prepared the food.

The fire had died down and was now glowing. The meal had been eaten, and Josh had his coffee. They decided that the fire should continue throughout the night. It was a necessity as the temperature dropped.

Making certain that it wasn't a flaming beacon of light but just a warm glow took a considerable amount of time and effort. As Josh sat on one side of the fire with his back against a rock—coffee cup in hand, and stomach full after the meal—he thought about the man and his rock carving.

"What do you reckon that guy was doing?" he said into the growing darkness. Amy, on the other side of the fire, could only be seen as a dark shape. Josh sensed, rather than saw, her lift her cup to her mouth and take a swallow of coffee before answering him.

"Do you remember Ben telling us about the article he read in the newspaper about a group of Southerners seeking to reinstate the South's Confederate government?" Amy asked Josh.

"Yes, some sort of circle, a secret society seeking to gain funds to start an insurrection," answered Josh.

"I think that man was carving a sign to a hidden cache of money or weapons. Didn't Pa say that Jesse James and some other thieves were taking the money for that secret circle?" Amy said.

"Could it be Jesse James is not hiding out in Devil's Mountain after all? He's come here with a definite purpose. All that money and gold he has stolen is going to be hidden away, ready for use by those traitors." Josh drained his tin cup of coffee, and reached for the pot again. "Another, Amy?" He lifted the pot in the air and shook it, realising that there was very little left

He heard Amy's chuckle from the other side of the fire: "You'd be upset if I said yes and took the last of the coffee."

Josh didn't reply to that. He was too busy pouring out the dregs. Leaning back against the rock, he tried to make himself comfortable. He held the cup in both hands, relishing the warmth between his fingers. He thought hard but could come to no conclusion. "I don't know what to make of it, but I know we need to take care. Your father was wrong. The bandits are not up near the tall peaks of Devil's Mountain, at least not all of them. We've just found one, and it was sheer luck we didn't ride in on top of him. But it makes life harder for us. We've to take extra care, Amy. We're not alone out here. Tomorrow, whatever we do, we must be on our guard. There are too many people wandering around Lonesome Creek canyon for my liking."

CHAPTER FOURTEEN

The horses watered and fed, Josh stood looking up at the boulder they were hoping to climb. It was perched on a rocky outcrop halfway up one of the jagged peaks of Devil's Mountain range.

"That's going to be a steep trail. There's no way the horses can manage that. It's far too steep for them." He looked around, seeing far more clearly by the light of the early morning the canyon and the creek rushing along it, full and almost overflowing after the rain.

Amy had joined him. The ends of her braids were dripping water from the creek. Washing her face had been not without difficulty. The powerful strength of the gushing water had made them both nervous: getting too close and falling in was not a desirable prospect. Without realising it, Amy's braids had dipped in whilst she was bent over. Josh watched her as she, too, looked up at the peak above them. The boulder they were aiming for was only halfway up, but it was not a straightforward task.

The sun lit up Amy's auburn hints in her brown hair and played across the freckles on her face as she screwed up her nose against its glare. Being with Amy alone for this length of time had shown Josh how comfortable they were together and how at ease he felt with this girl. There were no awkward pauses, never any difficult confrontations between them, nor any petty arguments. But Josh took himself to task. Now was not the time to ponder upon his relationship with Amy. Now was a time for action, with circumspection ensuring both their safety and the success of Luke's dream.

"It's the horses I'm worried about. We have to leave them—but where will they be safe?" Josh said, wondering if Amy had any thoughts on this problem.

Amy looked down at the canyon and then up towards the boulder. Then she looked back at their last night's camp. "Look over where we spent the night. I think the ledge continues along past the bushes. We didn't see that, because it was getting dark when we reached it. If it does, that would be an ideal place to tether the horses, giving them grazing and security. Let's look," said Amy.

They retraced their footsteps, returning to the evening's camp. Amy pushed past the bushes, thrusting them aside as she slid close to the wall of rock towering above them. At a particularly fierce bush with spiky branches, Amy paused.

Josh stepped forward and took his knife from his belt. "Here, I've got a knife. Let me cut some of those branches back. That way we'll get past, and it will give more room for the horses." He wielded his knife, and Amy stepped back to give him more room.

"You're right, Amy: there is more room past the bushes. If we hack some of them back, the horses will get in here and we can leave them and all our provisions hidden away and safe from prying eyes," said Josh. Energetically, he began hacking back some of the more obstructive branches. Satisfied with this arrangement, he helped Amy as they coaxed the horses back up and along to the opening underneath an overhanging ledge.

"No one will see them from down below. It will free us up, without our bags, to climb up to that wretched boulder," Amy muttered. Taking the water canteen and checking her gun, she stood ready for the ascent.

"It's not as steep as I thought," Josh panted as they neared the boulder. Taken slowly, the climb had been tedious and difficult. Manoeuvring around boulders and clambering over misshapen rocks had been tiring and strained all their muscles, as in some places they had to use their hands to clamber up the narrow track-like paths. "But it's far more tiring, and so difficult underfoot with all the loose rocks."

Amy had followed him, and he had heard her behind him rather than saw her. He knew by the sounds that she was close on his heels. There had been no need to look around and check. Anyway, Josh didn't have the energy to spare to check on Amy. It took all his energy to climb up beside the boulder. There, he sat down and reached a hand to help Amy clamber up the last cliff to the plateau, where the boulder with its hole sat.

"Thanks, Josh," she gasped. Taking huge breaths and placing her hands on her hips, Amy bent over, breathing deeply to fill her lungs. "That was hard," she whispered, finally finding the breath to speak again. She sat down beside him.

Neither of them jumped up to look through the hole. They were too exhausted. They sat, sipping the water from their canteens, and slowly their breath returned to normal.

"I suppose we better get up and see if what we came for is here," Josh said as he replaced the top of his canteen.

"Do we have to? I'm frightened to look through it. All this effort, and there may be no sign that my father was correct in his map readings. Josh, you get up and look first," Amy said, still sitting staring at the canyon beneath them.

Josh got up, bent over and put his hand out towards Amy. "Come on, Amy, we'll look together—and if there's nothing there, we'll go back and tell your father together."

Amy looked up at him, and Josh could see the gratitude in her eyes. And, for a moment, he felt certain there was something more in that look. Then it was gone, and Amy put out her hand and gave him her normal cheerful grin.

"Together, Josh, you're right. I can cope with this if we do it together. Let's look through that wretched hole and see where it leads."

CHAPTER FIFTEEN

The gaping chasm in the boulder was far greater than they'd expected. At waist height, the bottom of the rock rose in a circle above their heads and stretched through the entire boulder for some considerable way. Amy pressed her hands down onto the gnarled rock. The coarse texture, warm from the sun's rays, made it feel almost alive beneath her fingers. For one eerie moment, Amy felt the very rock pulsating at her touch. Ignoring the feeling, she stared straight ahead. The boulder was as large as the homestead at Broken Horseshoe Ranch and was balanced precariously on a rocky outcrop over the valley floor.

"That ledge over the canyon not only gives a vantage point up above Lonesome Creek but shows another canyon and valley breaking off sharply to the right from Lonesome Creek. You could only see this other canyon once you got down there on the canyon floor and went around those rocks. That canyon is stretching along the far foothills of Devil's Mountain," said Josh. He pointed it out to Amy.

"But look, Josh: immediately facing us on that ridge. Look! There's a cave. You wouldn't see it if you were standing down below. It can only be seen from this boulder." An increasing excitement seemed to take hold of Amy as she stood staring at this unexpected outcome of their climb. Amy grabbed Josh's arm and shook it. "Pa was right! You had to look through the boulder itself before you could see that cave. He's right, and he's reading the maps correctly now."

Josh put his hand on Amy's shoulder. "There's no other option, is there?"

"What do you mean, Josh?" Amy turned to look at the

man standing beside her. He was looking across at the cave with a wry smile on his lips and a look of determination on his face.

"What I mean, Amy, is that your old man has got us moving further forward with his quest. Now we have reached the boulder and climbed up to look through it, we have a further journey in front of us. We have to go up to that wretched cave! Can you imagine his fury if we go back without looking into it? I reckon he'd send us back out immediately!" Josh said and laughed at Amy's suddenly downcast face.

One last look at the cave opening and Amy shook her head. "You're right, Josh. Is it awful of me to wish we'd never seen that cave?" Amy turned to look at the journey back down to the horses. "It's as well I brought plenty of beans and bacon with me," she said and began the tortuous trek down the steep hillside.

Scrambling down the rocky terrain was surprisingly hard. "I thought the climb up to the boulder would be difficult, but coming down is even worse," grumbled Josh. The rocks, tiny at this point, were slipping beneath his feet as he put his foot down on them. "Just as I think I have a firm grip on the rocks to steady me, the boulders roll away from my grasp."

"Why is it so difficult to get down the hill?" moaned Amy. At one particularly steep point, she had resorted to going backwards, in a peculiar crab-like motion. "It's no good. I'm going to stop for a moment. I need to catch my breath."

Halfway through the descent, they found a small outcrop on which they could stand side by side and take some breaths and a drink. Neither of them had discussed their findings when they looked through the boulder, but both felt that would come when they had finished their climb down. They had no spare breath for any sort of discussion. Again, they looked around at the fantastic views of Devil's Mountain to one side, rearing up into the sky; and, at the end of the canyon of Lonesome Creek, further mountains could be seen reaching far into the distance.

"Look, what's that moving down there?" Amy pointed, knowing that they were safely hidden up on the hillside, with the vegetation shielding them from view. "I think it's that greasy man."

"The greasy man?" Josh asked, puzzled by her remark.

"Yes, the one trying to carve into the rock. He had a greasy hat and a greasy jacket. So, I call him the greasy man," Amy said, her full attention focused on the figure who was leading his horse into cover. As he tethered his horse, he reached for his rifle, bringing it around and walking out of the trees with it pointing in front of him.

It was Amy who spotted the Apache family first. "Look Josh, at the ancient cave dwellings. I think it's Sam and his family. They are coming down the hillside, away from their hiding place."

At this point in their descent, Amy, and Josh were on a level with the cliff dwellings. Some distance away, across the canyon level with them, the figures could be seen making their way down a narrow tortuous path to the canyon floor below them.

"I can't see Sam's horse. He must have stashed it somewhere down in the canyon. That must be his mother and brother. Not sure about the others—there's a group of five of them, but they seem to be going further along the canyon, away from Sam," Amy said, and she placed her hand over her eyes, shielding them from the sun to see

Sam's family.

"Greasy man has seen them. He's going to attack them! That's why he stopped to get his rifle. We must warn Sam! His family is in danger," Josh said, his face grim as he stared down at the man watching the Apache, who walked towards the man. They were unaware of the danger that was stalking them.

CHAPTER SIXTEEN

"Look! Amy! Along the ledge, towards the junction of all the canyons! There's an overhang above both canyons: Lonesome Creek Canyon, where the greasy man is stalking them, and the other canyon, beneath the ancient village. He's going to lie in wait for them there."

Josh grabbed Amy by the hand and led her towards the beginning of a perilous ledge on the rock face. "Hurry, Amy! If we reach that overhang, maybe we can stop him somehow. It's the only chance that Sam has. Otherwise, that man will shoot them. They won't know he's coming because they can't see him, but he, looking up, spotted them."

Amy began sidling onto the narrow ledge behind him. "How will we stop him? He'll see us and shoot us first, and then Sam." Taking one hesitant step after another, Amy grabbed branches of scrubby bits of vegetation and the jutting-out rocks that promised a precarious hold along the ledge.

Josh followed her. The difficulty they were facing took all their concentration. They could only think of where the next foothold or handhold would be. Far below them, the rocks lay tumbled and scattered along the canyon floor. One unwary step would mean certain death.

"I don't know, Amy. All I know is that we had better get along this ledge before that man reaches Sam. Once there, we'll think of something," Josh said. What he would think of, he had no idea. Josh knew they needed to reach the junction of the canyons before the greasy man hiding with his rifle killed Sam and his family.

Josh was struggling—and then he stopped moving. Amy, to her horror, saw the colour drain from his face.

He had been placing one foot slowly after another whilst searching for handholds. He had reached an unexpected hazard where the actual ledge petered out. A large boulder had fallen onto it, blocking their path. Josh had taken one look at this rocky giant and froze.

"I can't ... I can't ..." was all that he could manage through tight lips, his face and body pressed into the rock as he shook uncontrollably.

Amy, at that moment, felt utterly helpless. Josh was always so self-reliant and could always cope with anything life threw at him. Now, Amy realized, Josh was afraid of heights. She crept along the ledge and reached out to him, pressing her hand over his: "It's all right, Josh. I've got hold of you. I'm going to climb past you, around that boulder, and then help you onto the next bit of the ledge. Once there, it's so much easier. The ledge is much wider and we don't need to sidle alongside the cliff face."

Amy felt Josh's quivering body beneath her, as she slowly placed one foot between his two feet whilst manoeuvring past him. Her breath came in nervous, shallow gasps because she had to be so careful that she didn't knock both of them down to the boulder-strewn valley floor beneath them. Her hand grabbed a secure hold past the boulder. With an overwhelming relief, her first foot was placed upon the wider ledge. When past Josh, and securely placed upon the ledge, she put a hand under his elbow and guided him around that boulder. All the time, she was murmuring, "Keep going, Josh; keep going, Josh; you're almost there."

It seemed to take hours, but it wasn't even seconds before they both stood breathless on the wider expanse of ledge. Josh was panting but, to Amy's relief, she could see the colour coming back into his face.

"Sorry, Amy, I'm so sorry," Josh whispered, still panting for breath after his experience. Movement beneath them alerted them both back to the danger that Sam's family was walking into. Josh and Amy were now level with the man, but above him. He did not know that they were there, and they crept along the ledge above him and out onto the overhang.

"Sam," whispered Josh, and pointed. Sam was guiding his mother and talking to her and his young brother. Meanwhile, the man had taken up position, with his rifle, behind a large bush. He was directly beneath them and had his back to them. Josh looked around. Perhaps there was a boulder he could throw at the man. Perhaps he could shout, he thought—but that would only alert greasy man to their presence. There was nothing to stop the greasy man from killing both of them, and then Sam and his family. The man had a long-range weapon; they had only their guns.

Josh was wondering what to do, and he watched as, unknowingly, Sam was walking ever closer to danger. Josh felt Amy move beside him, and she drew out her knife from her pocket. Amy took it out of the home-made sheath she had made for it. Fashioned so it fitted neatly into her pocket, the knife was her ever-present companion.

"Move over, Josh. Let me get a better position. I think this is the only way, don't you?" Amy said, and held up the knife, showing Josh that she should throw it at the man.

Josh thought rapidly. If she missed, it would alert him to their presence. That would at least draw his attention away from Sam. He and Amy could draw back towards the cliff face behind them. Hopefully, the man's rifle would be useless then. Greasy man might find them out of his sight. And, if Amy killed him outright, the problem would be solved. Josh realized that while he had been thinking, Amy was still standing with her knife poised, ready for action. She was waiting for his decision.

"Yes Amy—throw your knife."

CHAPTER SEVENTEEN

Amy stared at Josh, the knife in her hand. The questioning in her eyes was met by a reassuring smile from him: "Now, Amy. Throw it now!"

Josh thought that even if Amy missed greasy man, the knife appearing from out of nowhere would startle him and make him take cover. The other advantage of the thrown knife was that the man would not know which direction it came from, so ensuring that their position would not be jeopardized. Greasy man's head was turned away from them, his eyes fixed on the approaching family through the bush.

A deep breath, her hand steady, Amy took aim at the man. Fortunately for her, he had paused behind the bush, ready to attack Sam. Crouched he was keeping still, obviously fearful that any movement would stir the bushes and alert Sam. Amy felt the weight of the knife in her hand. It had become familiar to her. The knife itself was an old one, given to her by Ezra and sharpened to a lethal point.

On her arrival at Broken Horseshoe Ranch, Amy knew the skills essential for living in an eastern town, skills she had learned as a young girl about to become a lady. Amy had been taught to embroider, paint an elegant watercolour, and write a fine letter. She knew how to curtsy, how to walk and sit with grace, and—most important of all—how to drink tea from a fine bone china teacup. Her sewing meant that she could make her own pretty dresses. No one had ever imagined that Amy would use that skill to fashion a sheath for a deadly weapon: her knife.

At Broken Horseshoe Ranch, none of those ladylike skills were of any use whatsoever. Amy was living in a whole new world and had to learn how to cope with the weather, the heat, and the discomfort of living in such a basic fashion. Having an elderly father and a much younger brother meant it had fallen upon Amy to learn how to live and exist and thrive in this new land. If she hadn't done it, no one else would, and the family would not have survived. Holding a gun, throwing a knife, and riding a horse were all new experiences to the girl. And they had to be learnt and mastered if the Tanner family was going to cope with Western life. Ezra and Leah, the elderly couple that Amy and her family had found living in a small cabin behind the ranch, helped the family to settle into the harsh environment. It was Ezra who took Amy to one side, and he spent many hours coaching the girl in the essentials the old man felt she needed for her new frontier life. Knife throwing had been one of Ezra's favourite skills and, finding an apt pupil in Amy, he had delighted in her progress.

Now, Ezra's words echoed in Amy's head as she readied herself to throw the knife. Amy lifted the knife and threw it. Josh watched the blade fly through the air. Amy's arm dropped at her side and she moved closer to Josh as they watched it reach its target and land between the man's shoulder blades. Without a sound, he fell to the rocky ground and tumbled beside the bush. His rifle fell, unheeded by the man—now dead on the ground.

"Well done, Amy! That was an excellent throw!" Josh's jubilant voice made Amy smile. Amy felt delighted that her ability had saved Sam and his family—*and* saved herself and Josh. But she looked down at the man lying still on the ground. There could be no doubt about it: the man was dead, and by her hand. Amy felt a twinge of horror that she had been the one to destroy the man's life, even a man as evil as he had been.

"Don't think about it, Amy. You *had* to kill him. Anything else would have meant death for Sam and his family, and us. It had to be done." Josh's words took much of the horror away from Amy. Yes, she knew it had to be done, but never would she rejoice in the death of a man. And she hated to think that he had died by her hand.

"Come on, Amy! Let's climb down and meet Sam."

CHAPTER EIGHTEEN

The rocks were hot to the touch and the sun, now high in the sky, was glaring down on them. The heat was building up as they stood high above the canyon with no shade. Josh longed to escape that rock face, but the thought of leaving the security of the ledge they were standing on scared him. He stood looking down towards the dead man, at Sam and his family coming nearer to them, and still he was frightened, and didn't want to move.

"Josh, it's easier going down this way. Look, if we go to the side, there is almost a path down to the canyon floor. It's not nearly as tricky as that last climb along the ledge." Walking to the far side of the ledge, Amy reached out for Josh's hand: "Come on, I'll guide you down."

Josh knew he had to move; he couldn't stay there all day. He took a deep breath and walked towards Amy, his teeth clenched hard, and reached out his hand to her. "You'll help me down?" His voice was the merest whisper, and he stood in front of her, staring at her, never looking down at the sheer drop below.

"Josh, take my hand and put one hand against the rock face. All we have to do is just walk down this narrow, winding path. I'm telling you, Josh, it's not like that last climb we did along the rock face. This is so much easier." Amy held out her hand and took one step down onto the path.

One eye squinted at the path, and then Josh examined it closely. He wasn't going to look down. No, he wasn't that foolish, "Oh Amy, you're right. It's far easier. I thought you were just being kind to me."

Taking one hand, Amy urged Josh onto the path. They

proceeded one step at a time and with one hand on the rock face to give them the security on the ledge as it sloped downwards. Amy looked down at Josh's bowed head, at his hair that glinted golden in the sunlight. He was fixedly staring down at the path, at each step that he took with infinite care. Not once did his eyes slide sideways to the drop below to the canyon floor. In all their journeys through Devil's Mountain, Amy had never realized the fear that he must have held bottled up inside whenever they climbed anywhere. It took some bravery, thought Amy, to carry on round that enormous boulder when he froze, and now to continue going down the path.

"We're on the bottom now, Josh. You've done it!" Amy laughed at Josh's surprised face.

Josh looked round, and his eyes widened. "I made it! Thanks to you, Amy. I don't know what came over me. How could I possibly get in such a state as I did on that climb?" He turned round to look up at the boulder that had caused him so much grief. It jutted out from the cliff and straddled over onto the narrow ledge that they had been climbing along. "It *was* a large boulder, wasn't it?" Josh stared up at it, astonished at how Amy had manoeuvred him around it. He shuddered: the fear he'd felt—and utter helplessness that had overwhelmed him—would not be easily forgotten.

"Josh, what are you doing here? Hello Amy, are you here as well?" Sam's cheerful voice, as he walked towards them, made them both smile. He had been unaware of the drama concerning his approach towards them, and his family's descent from the cliff village.

It was Matthew, his younger brother, who spotted the fallen man lying beside the bush, his rifle beside him.

"He was lying in wait for you—but Amy dispatched

him," Josh said as he walked towards the family group. They congregated round the fallen man.

"Turn him over, Matthew. Let's see if we know him," said Sam.

They watched as the young boy pulled the knife out of the man's back and handed it up to his brother. Then he pulled the man over so that they could see his face.

"Do you know him?" Josh asked Sam. "We saw him earlier. He was carving signs into a rock. He didn't see us, and we continued on our way. Then we saw he had you and your family in his sights and was hiding behind the bush, ready to ambush you."

Sam, whilst listening, had—without thinking—cleaned the blood off Amy's knife with a handful of grass. He handed it to the girl, with a murmured thanks and a look of intense admiration.

Amy took the knife and shuddered slightly as she remembered what had just happened, and where it had been. But she placed it back into its sheath and into her pocket. She smiled her thanks at the tall man who was standing over her.

Sam nodded and smiled down at her. Josh caught the look on Sam's face as Amy turned to speak to Sam's mother. Unaware of Josh's scrutiny, there had been a moment that passed fleetingly over Sam's face. That moment revealed to Josh the love that Sam felt for Amy. The tall, handsome half-breed's face instantly shifted to its usual impassive expression. There was no way that Josh had mistaken that expression on Sam's face. Sam was in love with Amy.

CHAPTER NINETEEN

"His horse is back here," Matthew called to the others, finding the horse tethered to a small tree. He led it back to the group.

Meanwhile, both Josh and Sam squatted down beside the man and began emptying his pockets. There was very little to show for the man's life. The only thing of interest was a small piece of paper with a couple of signs drawn on it, and they also discovered a folded sheet with a roughly drawn map of Lonesome Creek on it.

"That's the huge rock he was carving the signs on. The next two crosses must show two more rocks to be carved," said Josh, smoothing out the papers and showing them to the others.

"Why did he want to kill us? What harm had we ever done to him?" Hannah, Sam's mother, whispered the words, almost as if she knew there could be no answer. The man saw them coming down from the village and had just decided to kill them. She turned and impulsively wrapped an arm around Amy. "Thank you, my dear. I know how hard it was for you to do this. But you had to kill him, to save all our lives."

Amy felt the warmth coming from the other woman and smiled gratefully at her. Her understanding of how Amy actually felt over the man's death, and the part she played in it, was heartwarming.

Matthew, beside the horse, had been investigating the saddle bags. Apart from the usual cowboy gear every rider carried with him, Matthew found a leather pouch containing papers: "This has some sort of a wax seal on it. I'll open it, shall I?"

Before anyone could answer, the boy's curiosity won

out, and he tore open the seal and opened it. "There're many documents in here. They must be important to have a seal on them. I wonder who he was taking them to—or do you think he stole them?" Matthew said, and handed them to Josh, who was standing nearest to him.

Sam was still down beside the dead man. He undid the man's belt buckle and drew it out with the gun still in its holster. He put it beside the rifle and then stood up. "We'll bury him, of course. Let's place him under those trees."

The task was done and, after washing their hands and brushing the dust and dirt from their trousers, the men joined Amy and Hannah, who were seated on a large rock beside the creek.

"Sam, you have your horse tethered at the entrance to Lonesome Creek canyon. Take this other horse too, and get your family to Dry Creek Ranch. Nancy is there and expecting you. Tell her we'll be back tomorrow, and then we can take the documents into the town and give them to the sheriff," Amy said.

"What about the man's gun? And his rifle? And his provisions?" Matthew asked, looking at the man's goods lying beside the women.

"We don't need them," Josh said, and looked at Sam. "I suggest you take those to the ranch. Oh, wait a minute! We'll take his coffee—we're running out."

Amy smiled; Josh loved his coffee as much as her father did; his concern that morning, when he realized they were running low on coffee, had been funny. Now she wouldn't have to put up with his complaining about the lack of coffee.

"If you don't need them Josh, I reckon my young brother could do with them, especially the gun. This land is so dangerous; it's best he's armed too."

They had all drunk and eaten the few provisions they had amongst them, leaving Josh and Amy enough for overnight and in the morning.

"My grandson, David? How is he, Amy?" Hannah asked Amy.

Amy smiled at the older woman and at her anxious expression as she thought of the little boy. "Your grandson is growing bigger each day. He laughs a lot and is great friends with my dog, Meg. Leah and Nancy take turns in watching and playing with him. He loves it when the boys are with him. Both Chan and Tom make excellent babysitters. I'm afraid my brother gets lost in his books, so he is never left alone with him."

"There are so many of you to watch out for him. That is so good. I should like to see him," Hannah said wistfully.

"Of course you will see him. We'll work it out that you see him as soon as possible," Amy promised. Hannah's eyes lit up with joy as Amy told of the little boy's escapades around Broken Horseshoe Ranch.

CHAPTER TWENTY

When Sam and his family left them it was still early afternoon, and Josh and Amy agreed that there was time to reach the cave before nightfall

With a renewed enthusiasm, Amy and Josh began climbing towards the cave set midway up the opposite range of hills to those of Lonesome Creek canyon.

Standing at the foot of the cliff face and checking that they had all they needed, Amy had smiled at Josh, who noticed her careful appraisal of the height and difficulty of the climb: "It's not too bad; it's not difficult at all."

Her reassurance helped Josh. She had worked that out for herself, and was facing the climb with an overwhelming eagerness to find out exactly what was in that cave. "I hope there's something there. After all our effort and my father's hopes, it would be good to find something. Anything!" Amy strode on up the rocky terrain, eager to get on with the search.

"What did you make of those papers that Matthew found? I didn't study them. But they seemed to be worth a second look, don't you agree?" Josh said. "That man must have been a messenger of some sort. Those papers were important to someone, especially having them tightly closed with a special wax seal."

Amy paused and stared at Josh, thinking carefully over her words before speaking again. "I saw a few headings written about the Confederates, and there was mention of collecting money for a special fund. I think they need looking at carefully to understand their full importance. Sheriff Grey is the one we should give them to. Let him sort them out. That man was evil. I'd rather we had nothing more to do with any of his things."

Amy's voice became hard and unlike her usual gentle self. Thinking over her words as they continued the climb, Josh found himself in agreement with her: "You're right, I'd rather we had nothing more to do with him, and whatever he was involved in. Best we know nothing about it."

It seemed a tiring journey, clambering up the rocky hillside. Josh realized they were both tired and still suffering from that hazardous journey across the rock face to save Sam and his family. The heat of the day was increasing their discomfort and, although they had rested beside the creek, for a while, they were still tired.

"Not far to go now. I hope there are not too many chests of jewels and gold coins—I'm too tired to carry them," said Josh. Exhaustion, both emotionally and physically, had made him feel he had to lighten the mood between them. Anything to keep their spirits going.

"Yes, you're quite right, Josh. Caskets of gold and silver coins, and chests of jewels, would be far too heavy to carry today. But if there's a jewelled tiara and an emerald necklace, and perhaps a string of pearls, I could wear them. That wouldn't be too bad. Of course, if there were rings, you could always put them on each finger." Amy added her silliness to the conversation. It helped to lighten the tired feeling that was becoming overwhelming. They soon reached the entrance to the cave, both smiling at their silly remarks to each other.

This side of the canyon was in shadow, the sun never reaching this point. They walked along the narrow entrance in front of the cave and peered in. A strong, musty odour seemed to linger around the entrance, but they could see nothing because the dark impenetrable shadow hid all within it.

Slung over his shoulder and across his body, Josh carried a canvas bag. Pulling it round towards him, he opened it and walked over to a convenient rock and placed on it a candle and tinderbox. Josh and Amy had learned the hard way that bringing a light was essential before entering the cave.

Whilst he did this, Amy had walked around the ledge and was searching for other clues. There was nothing, and she walked back towards him, shaking her head.

Josh held the candle, shielding it from the wind with his other hand, and walked towards the cave entrance. Amy was beside him. Almost without conscious thought, she pulled her gun from her pocket and readied it to fire. A quizzical look from him, first at her and then at the gun, made her laugh.

"One of Ezra's sayings: never walk into a cave unprotected. You don't know what might be in there— and it may well object to your visit and attack you," said Amy.

"Oh well, if Ezra said it, I agree it's worthwhile. That man knows these mountains like the back of his hand. Well, we made it, Amy. Now we see if it was worth our while," Josh said, proceeding further into the cave.

"Be careful, Josh. Remember the booby-trapped mine? The Jesuits are renowned for playing tricks when hiding treasure. We know that of old. So, take it slowly and carefully."

CHAPTER TWENTY-ONE

Their footsteps made a shushing sound as they took their time, placing one step in front of the other. The dust was thick and swirled around their ankles, the smell a strange mixture of dead things. They knew they had to tread carefully, looking around constantly for any booby traps.

"I don't trust those Jesuits. Remember, they booby-trapped that last cave we went in? If it hadn't been for Ezra, we would both be dead by now. But I can't see anything that would be dangerous to us, can you, Amy?" Josh said, moving the candle from side to side slowly, with his other hand shielding it from the breeze coming from the cave entrance.

"There's nothing here, and it looks as if no animals have even slept in it," Amy said, following Josh then moving to the side of him, but still taking care to be within the glow from the candlelight.

Another step Josh took, and another. Now they were halfway into the cave itself and, when he held the candle aloft, he could see its back wall. "It's not big, is it? It seems fairly open and there are no hidden passages. Why would they have led us here? Is it another mischievous joke by those Jesuits, another trick to lead us astray and stop us from searching?"

He had reached the back wall of the cave, and they could see that the rock itself was the floor of the cave and had only dust, twigs, and ancient leaves blown into it. Eddies of wind would swirl around the cave in the many storms that frequented Devil's Mountain. The wind's passage was evident in the strange piles of dust caught in the rock walls.

It was Amy, following on behind Josh but turning

closer to the wall, who found it. At first she thought it was another pile of dust, swirled into a peculiar shape, in a crevice in the rock wall. She walked nearer to it, still taking care, still placing each foot deliberately and glancing around for any tripwires or booby traps.

"Josh, bring the candle over here! I think I've found something!" The mounting excitement in Amy's voice alerted Josh even before her words fell upon his ears. He strode back towards her, the candle quivering in the hasty rush of air.

"What is it? What do you think you've found?" Beside her now, he too dropped and squatted beside her. Amy pointed a shaking finger towards the heap of dirt in small depression in the rock floor and wall.

"I can't see anything. What can you see, Amy?" Josh asked her, excitement now gripping him.

"I saw the candlelight make something shine in that pile of dust. Hold the candle nearer to it. I think it's some sort of metal. Can you see it, Josh? Look, it's down there."

Josh followed Amy's pointing finger, holding the candle closer to the mound of dirt in the dusty crevice. He swore sharply. At the moment's excitement, he'd forgotten the candle was full of melting wax, which had now run onto his hand. Quickly changing hands, he continued looking closely. Spotting a stick nearby, he lifted it and began gently clearing some of the dirt from the object.

"It's a buckle! I think it's a silver buckle. That's what was shining in the candlelight," said Amy.

"Amy, you're right. It's a buckle, and look, it's a leather bag. Here, Amy, you hold the candle and I'll try to remove it. I think you should stand up and get ready to run out of the cave when I grab it. You never know what'll happen when I grab it. The movement may set off something. Look, I've removed all the dust, I see a strap. I'm going to grab the strap of the bag and run to the entrance of the cave. You go first, Amy. Go now!"

Amy needed no second bidding. She remembered a time when not only the roof collapsed when a trigger was activated, but the floor as well. And the entire cave came down around them. If it hadn't been for Ezra urging them out of the cave before the actual collapse happened, they would all have been dead.

She ran out to the cave entrance, moved to the side, and awaited Josh's arrival. He was beside her almost immediately, clutching the leather bag in one hand.

It was a small bag, ingrained with dirt, and the silver buckle holding the flap closed was what Amy had spotted. Josh held it in his hand and looked at Amy: "Do we open it now?"

CHAPTER TWENTY-TWO

"Or should we go down below, set up camp, and then open it?" Josh looked down at the small, dusty leather bag in his hand. He turned it over and then fingered the buckle.

"I'm desperate to open it now," admitted Amy, "but this side of the canyon is already in shadow, and the light is fading fast. I think we should get off this cliff while we still have daylight. Josh, you are being very sensible. We should set up camp for the night ahead." Amy put out a finger, touched the bag gently, then prodded the silver buckle she had spotted. "Yes, after we set up camp; we'll open it then."

The bag was placed in Josh's canvas satchel, which was still lying on top of the rock. Josh's candle stub was placed in it with the tinderbox. Not weighing much, Josh wondered just what the bag actually contained. It was a thought that struck Josh and quite depressed him. What did the bag contain? It can't be anything of much value, he thought, not in that tiny bag and with no weight to it.

The journey down the cliff face was passed in silence, and they reached the bottom of the canyon with little light left on that side of it. Scrabbling down, they made use of the large boulders and scrubby vegetation in their path, both providing hand and foot holds. Hurrying now, desperate to gain what little light was left to them, they rushed towards their horses and the provisions and blankets they had left on the secluded ledge.

Josh took the horses down the river, whilst Amy lit a small fire and put the coffee pot on. That morning, they had finished the last of their coffee, but now she went into her own satchel and brought out the coffee that had been in the man's saddlebag. Amy hesitated as she looked at it but then she shrugged. After all, he wouldn't need it, so they might as well have it. But as she got it ready, and put the coffee pot on the fire, Amy said a prayer for the man and his eternal soul. Somehow, she knew it would make drinking his coffee seem so much better to her.

In no time at all they had the makings of a meal, eaten sitting beside the small fire on the ledge in Lonesome Creek canyon. The horses were none the worse for their enforced rest, and Amy felt Bella had enjoyed the grazing and resting.

It was no wonder that both of them gobbled their food; it was no wonder they cleared their plates and sorted out their bedrolls ready for the night at an amazing speed. Then, and only then, did Josh place the leather bag on a flat stone beside them.

"From the weight of it, and the size of the bag, I don't think, Amy, you're going to get your tiara and emerald necklace. I very much doubt that it's full of gold coins," Josh said as he pulled the strap through the silver buckle.

Amy drew closer to Josh, almost breathing down his neck. They both watched as the strap gradually came out through the buckle. The silver buckle was tarnished, almost black with age, and it was purely a fluke that Amy had spotted it in the dim candlelight.

Josh had the flap open. On a flat piece of rock in front of him, he shook out the contents. There was a clatter as some beads and a crucifix fell onto the rock. "It's a rosary," said Josh. He touched it with a finger and gave a disappointed sigh. "It's a wooden rosary."

"What else is in there, Josh? Is there anything else? Shake it out!" Amy pulled at his sleeve, impatient to find out what else was in the bag.

Josh shook the upended bag and a crucifix fell out, larger than the one on the rosary, but again it was made of wood. "The figure looks as if it's silver, but it's so tarnished with age it's hard to be certain." Shaking the bag one last time, and upending it even more, Josh watched as a scroll of paper fell out onto the rock.

"That's it? Surely that's not all? Look again, Josh. I'm sure there must be something else inside that bag." Amy's disappointed remarks seemed to echo in the dark night around them. She couldn't believe it: how they had worked so hard to find the cave and then to find the bag with nothing in it. Well, nothing much of value, Amy thought,

The bag was now fully open and Josh put his hand down into each corner, carefully searching for something else. Anything that would make this journey, and their search, have been worthwhile. "Nothing—there's nothing else in the bag. Nothing!"

CHAPTER TWENTY-THREE

When the fire died down, Josh or Amy took turns to put some of the wood (they had found earlier) on the embers to keep it alight. Neither of them could sleep, and neither of them wanted the darkness to descend completely. Their thoughts were upon the bag and its contents. This endless pursuit of Jesuit gold was not only tiring physically, but it had also become emotionally draining, especially for Amy. She knew how much her father depended on their bringing back further clues for him to achieve his lifetime dream.

Luke wanted the gold for his children—a legacy he could leave for them. His greatest wish was for Ben to go back east and attend college. Their abrupt removal to Broken Horseshoe Ranch had disrupted Ben's schooling, which worried Luke. There was no money available at the moment to send him back east, but if the gold was found not only could Ben then go and be educated, but Amy could also return and find herself the young suitor she would have had if they'd remained in their old house in town.

"Are you awake, Amy?" Josh, sleeping on the other side of the fire to Amy, saw the creeping fingers of dawn above Devil's Mountain. He had heard the girl move restlessly throughout the night, because he too lay awake. The stars in the night sky were too many to even consider counting them. Lying on his back, he had stared in wonder at the vast expanse of night sky and the clarity of it. Now, seeing the approach of dawn, he thought if Amy was awake, it would be best to make an early start.

"Yes, Josh." Amy stretched out under her blanket, then she sat up, pulling it up round her chin and shivering.

"I've hardly slept, and I've heard you move around a lot."

"I thought you were awake. Shall we make an early start? If we have breakfast now, and see to the horses, it should be light enough for us to travel through the canyon. I'll see to the horses." Josh got up and rolled up his bedroll, then saddled up the horses before taking them down to the creek to drink.

Amy wrapped the blanket around her like a shawl. She was cold and still shivering. Then she stirred the fire up and got the coffee ready, putting the last of the bacon into the pan along with last night's leftover biscuits and beans. It would be good to get back to the ranch and have some of Tom's interesting Chinese-based vegetable dishes. Bacon and beans were filling, and exactly what was needed on a chilly morning, but they got boring.

Neither of them spoke about the bag until they were riding out of Lonesome Creek Canyon. "I hope Pa is not too disappointed. Maybe he'll find something of interest in that scroll. We never even bothered looking at it, did we?" Amy said.

"I felt cheated, didn't you, Amy? Nothing but the wooden rosary beads and crucifix. I really thought, after all our trouble to get up to that cave, and after reaching the boulder with a hole in it, that there would be something worthwhile," Josh said. "No doubt your father will find something of interest in the scroll. I'm sure he will find it informative. But I hope he doesn't send us off again looking for some more Jesuit gold."

"Oh yes, Josh—I hope he doesn't send us off again. I couldn't bear to look at the scroll last night. And you're quite right, Josh. I don't want to search for that wretched gold for some time. Do you know, Josh, those horrible accounts of Manuel seem more interesting to me now!"

Amy laughed at the idea that the accounts—which she moaned about constantly—could be preferable to hiking up and down hillsides and riding through canyons searching for gold.

Because of their early start, they made good time. The horses, left on their own for such a long time, had grazed and rested and were full of energy. They seemed to know they were returning home and the nearer they got to the ranch the more their speed increased. It was with a wonderful sense of relief that Josh and Amy rode under the Broken Horseshoe Ranch sign.

The waving figures of Ben, Tom, and Chan made them both laugh, and they waved back, pleased to be home. Leah stood beside them, holding the tiny figure of David, who was also waving at them. As they got nearer to the group, they could see they were all gathered round David, urging him to do something. It was only when they reached David that they realized what the excitement was all about.

Both Amy and Josh dismounted, and Leah held out David to the girl. "Go on, David, go on," the boys were urging him.

Then, as if realizing that it was Amy in front of him, he put out his chubby hands and arms and waved them furiously at her. "Amy! Amy!" he cried out, to the accompaniment of cheers by the others standing around. "Amy!"

CHAPTER TWENTY-FOUR

The delight on the chubby face of David at Amy's return made them all laugh. Amy took him in her arms and he clung to her neck as if he would never let her go. Surprised at the extent of his affection, and the open way in which David showed it, Amy cuddled the little boy close to her as she walked into the cabin.

At the table, she seated herself, with David on her knee. Ben and Chan raced off with the horses to the stable. "Wait for us! Don't start the story until we get back," they both shouted.

Tom helped Josh bring in their gear from their extended stay out in Lonesome Creek. The two important bags were placed on the table. They were looked at with great curiosity. But no one asked what was in them until both new arrivals were handed some coffee.

"Let me have my drink, David. Do you want to go down on the floor and play?" Amy asked the little boy, whose blond curls tickled her chin as he wriggled about on her knee. He shook his head and pulled the tiny rag toy he had arrived with from a pocket in the jacket that Leah had made for him, and began chewing it. Nestling back into her arms, he sat and chewed contentedly. Amy glanced down at him and smiled. The affection she felt for the tiny baby was overwhelming and, in some ways, frightening. He didn't belong to her and could leave Broken Horseshoe Ranch at any time. Sam and his mother could always claim him. *They* were his family after all, a thought that struck Amy with an unexpected pang. It would be hard to let him go now. She had grown so fond of David and, when he fell asleep in her arms, Amy realized *she* had become just as important to David.

Ben and Chan dashed in the door. "You haven't started, have you?" Both boys looked searchingly at Amy and then Josh. They both shook their heads, laughing at the accusing looks from the boys, who were out of breath from running and excitement.

Draining his coffee, Josh got up and went over to the stove and reached for the coffee pot. He lifted it up, looking around to see if anyone else would like a refill. At Luke's nod and lifting of his cup, Josh walked over, topped it up and then did the same with his own cup. He looked over at Amy. She shook her head, gesturing to the sleeping child in her lap. Josh nodded his understanding and, placing his cup on the table, he stretched his hand out for his satchel. There was a sigh of anticipation from those gathered around the table.

Josh began speaking as he pulled the satchel towards him and began opening it: "We had quite an eventful trip. We'll tell you all about it in due course. But first, I know Luke wants to know what happened in our treasure hunt. We went up to the boulder with a hole in it. When we got up there, we were astonished at the size of it. There was nothing to be seen around it. We found no signs or any disturbed earth. It was only when we looked through the actual hole itself that we could see, in the hillside directly opposite to us, there was a cave." Josh lifted his cup and took another drink of coffee. "This cave would not be seen from the ground, but only from our position of standing behind the boulder and looking through the hole."

There was an intense silence as every person in the room stared at him. Not one of them wanted to blink or move slightly. They were all rigid with suspense. "We spent the night there, knowing that to come back to

Broken Horseshoe Ranch without visiting that cave wouldn't be a popular move. Especially with Luke!" He smiled at Luke, who gave a short bark of laughter.

"You would've been sent back out, both of you, in a hurry!" was Luke's comment at this.

"Well, our journey up to the cave took longer than we expected. I'll tell you all about it later," Josh said hurriedly, catching the impatient glare from Luke. "It was a rocky cave, under an overhang of rock. It was small and narrow and full of dust and leaves. We scrabbled about and we finally found this in the corner."

The bag was drawn out of Josh's satchel and handed over to Luke. "Here it is, Luke. Sorry it's not gold or silver coins. Just a wooden rosary and a crucifix, and a scroll. We didn't bother opening the scroll; you can see it's still rolled up and tied with ancient cord."

Amy watched her father finger the wooden beads, then the crucifix. She was pleased that they hadn't opened the scroll. There had been little time for them to bother with it. She loved seeing the delight on her father's face as he got to open this new artefact by himself. The frustration he felt at being unable to search for the Jesuit treasure himself was usually well hidden. She recognized the frustration flaring briefly whenever his body failed him, hindering his search. This ancient scroll, still tied up, gave him at least the power of a new discovery in some small measure. Fingering the wooden artefacts one more time, he looked at them all. "You realize we are the first people to touch these since they were put there by the Jesuits themselves? Such a powerful link between us, it's almost as if we are in actual physical contact with them."

Amy understood and appreciated these words from her father. But, judging from the expressions on the faces of the three boys, they couldn't care less about this powerful link Luke was talking about. All they wanted was for Luke to open the scroll. Immediately!

Taking a knife, Luke cut the cord, and it fell onto the table in dirty, curling threads. The scroll itself he placed on the table. Holding the bottom carefully in place with one hand, he slowly proceeded to unroll it with the other. There were sharp indrawn breaths as it opened out. Each one of them stretched over the table, the nearer to see what was being revealed as the curling scroll opened before them. Slowly, taking the utmost care with the fragile document, Luke finally opened it, laying it flat on the table.

CHAPTER TWENTY-FIVE

"There's a heading, and the writing is in Spanish. Being Jesuits, I had expected them to write in Latin. It's another map. I think it's Lonesome Creek Canyon and ..." Luke stopped speaking. He began to say something, but stopped again. His eyes had widened, and it was almost as if he didn't know what to say. "And it looks like the map shows the land around Broken Horseshoe Ranch itself!" The words came out of Luke's mouth in a strange, strangled voice, as if spoken by someone else.

Josh dropped his cup on the table (luckily, he'd finished his coffee), and he rushed over to Luke's side. The older man pushed the scroll towards him, eager to get his opinion. Ezra also came to the other side of Luke, and he too stared down at the sprawling, spidery writing and the wavy lines that depicted the edge of Devil's Mountain, its foothills, and Lonesome Creek canyon and the land that spread out from it. That land contained Broken Horseshoe Ranch.

"What does that say?" Ezra pointed to the words. They were scrawled together and, somehow, they had been blotched; it was impossible to make them out.

"I don't know, Ezra. It's hard to decipher. What can that mean?" Luke replied to the older man, his finger tracing the signs and markings on the ancient scroll. "There's a circle beside it, not an X marking the spot. Ezra, can you work out the actual place that they are marking?" Luke pointed to the sign, shook his head, and repeated: "What can that mean? If only we could understand that, it would give us a clue."

Ben was now stretching over behind his father to look down at the map. His eyes were wide with excitement, and he stared again and again at the cryptic clues and marks on the scroll. Excitedly, he clapped his hands and began to dance a wild jig around the room. "This means we can search for the treasure. Josh and Amy aren't going to have all the fun! Pa, you and us three can get going at once to find the gold. Chan, Tom: you'll want to help too, won't you?"

The two Chinese boys grinned enthusiastically at Ben, both obviously eager at this news. Josh stared at the three boys and couldn't stop smiling back at them. Their enthusiasm and excitement echoed in the expression on Luke's face. His lined face, haggard with the pain and coughing that he was enduring daily, was gone for that moment. Only excitement and joy in the discovery were present.

"Oh dear, Amy, we're goin to have to share the fun that we have been having. We've enjoyed ourselves, especially on this last trip, haven't we?" Josh said to Amy.

Her appreciative smile at his sarcastic remark brought an answering smile to his face. Neither of them enjoyed their last trip, fraught with danger and death. Neither of them would have called it fun.

"Wonderful! We can dig buried treasure on our own land. Just think, Josh and Amy have been travelling all over the place and the very buried treasure they were searching for may have been all this time under the ..." Ben found he couldn't continue.

"Under the sweetcorn," said Chan with a grin.

"Under the stable," said Tom.

Amy put her hand up to halt the flow of likely hiding places "Enough, boys—you'll go on forever and you'll wake the baby. I really think this is an astonishing development. I've to agree with Ben: all our travelling, all the dangers we faced, and now the treasure may well be under our very feet. That's amazing." Amy shook her head at the strange turn of events that the scroll had brought to light.

"What's in that other bag?" Ben asked them, pointing to the bag with the broken wax seal that had also come out of Josh's satchel.

"This bag contains documents and papers." Josh stretched across the table and brought the bag in front of him. He placed a hand on it and looked round the room at everyone. His normally cheerful face became solemn, and he spoke in an unusually quiet voice which carried a note of authority, not without fear. "Not one person in this room must speak of what's in here. You must take the greatest care that knowledge of these papers does not come to the ears of anyone. I mean it! We didn't read them all thoroughly, but we saw enough to know that they are dangerous papers to have in our possession. They're linked to treason and plots against the government."

Josh took out the papers from the bag, with careful deliberation he placed them on the table in front of them. The scroll and the artefacts found in the Jesuit bag had been put to one side by Luke, placed on a shelf out of harm's way. They lay beside his usual chair, awaiting closer inspection

These papers contained lists resembling itemized financial accounts. Letters from various people had only a few names written; there were mainly initials. There was one document that had the heading of the Knights of the Golden Circle. This official-looking document was, in essence, a call to arms, and told of the stockpiling of gold, banknotes, and weapons ready for an insurrection against the present government. These documents stated that there was a plan in place for an uprising to bring the Confederacy not only back into power, but with an even greater power base formed by other states joining them.

"These are dangerous papers to have in our possession," said Josh.

The papers were passed around and Ezra, Leah, and Luke read them with increasing horror and fear. They passed them back to Josh, who placed them in a pile in front of him. The boys had glanced at them but, being so young, they meant little to them.

"First, I think these papers are significant and must get into the right hands as quickly as possible. They are documents that speak of Confederate plans and give details of where and how they are raising money for their cause. It gives the plans and motive for the utmost despicable treachery against our government." The solemnity of Luke's voice fell into the increasing horror that each of them was feeling at the sight of the documents, and the treachery portrayed within them.

CHAPTER TWENTY-SIX

David clung to Amy as she got ready to go to the general store that morning. He understood her going to the store for the day, but she'd been away for two nights and he didn't understand that it would not happen again. She reassured him, hoping that he understood what she meant. He stopped crying, but he still looked suspiciously at her as she got ready.

"I'm going to take these documents to the sheriff. He can deal with them. We won't tell Manuel or Eliza about it. Do you agree with that, Luke?" Josh said as he finished his coffee at the table. Tom had insisted they eat breakfast before they travelled into Nowhere. He had been worried about their lack of good food after their trip to Lonesome Canyon.

Amy had enjoyed the breakfast. Tom loved cooking and delighted in placing his efforts in front of everyone. Amy and Josh had shared the cooking on their trip, but it was Amy that hated preparing and cooking food. To have it cooked and served by Tom again was wonderful.

"Of course, we'll tell them all about the man who tried to bushwhack Sam and his family. I'll use that as my excuse to go up to speak to the sheriff," said Josh.

"I think that is the best way to deal with the problem," Luke said. He had joined them at breakfast; his health had been improving with the medicine Sam's tribal elder had made for him. But everyone knew that this morning Luke had risen early because he was keen to investigate the possibility of his Jesuit gold treasure actually being on Broken Horseshoe Ranch. "I'm going to draw out a copy of the map, with the landmarks we are familiar with on it. That way, we can investigate each marking of the original map and link it in with the ranch as it is now." Luke's enthusiasm and renewed interest had brought more colour into his face and, almost without thinking, he ate the breakfast Tom placed in front of him.

"Tom said that he would deal with the garden and all the cooking today. Then Chan and I can come and help you look for the sites you want to dig, Pa. Chan and I can carry things for you and dig out any promising places," Ben said, his offer of help not masking the excitement he felt at being able to unearth the Jesuit gold treasure on the ranch.

Amy, who had spent many days fruitlessly searching for treasure and been disappointed so many times, could only hope that her father and brother had better luck. She looked at Josh and saw on his face a similar expression to that which must've been on her own. Disappointment was an integral part of treasure hunting, and whilst her father and Ben had heard about their disappointing searches, they hadn't experienced them themselves.

Amy kept quiet. Why spoil her father's new and exciting interest? After all, he may well be lucky and find it in their first dig. She rose to her feet, kissed David goodbye, and handed him to Leah. Getting her satchel, she slid it over her shoulder and across her body, as usual. Her hand automatically went to one pocket in her skirt. Her knife was there. She didn't need to check the other pocket. She knew her gun, her usual Colt Peacemaker, was there: it's comforting weight was as familiar to her as her bandana tied around her neck. Her suede coat with the fringes was already shrugged on, and she walked out onto the porch. Ben had raced off to the stable and brought their buggy out for them.

Setting off for the town of Nowhere, after the few days

away from it, was familiar, and Amy felt pleasant. "I don't enjoy doing the accounts, but they are so much easier than climbing along ledges and up and down cliff faces," Amy said as they drove along the route to the town.

Josh mumbled his agreement. He was quiet on the journey, and Amy knew that the documents he was carrying worried him. She could only hope that when he had handed them over to the sheriff, and knew that someone in authority was dealing with them, he would relax.

The noise alerted them first: the constant banging and shouting seemed to drift across open spaces between the buggy and the township. Even at the distance they were away from it sudden snatches would reach their ears.

"What's going on? What on earth is all that noise?" Josh said, stretching up to peer ahead, shielding his eyes from the sun, hoping to catch a glimpse of whatever was happening in the town.

They approached Main Street, and the noise grew more distinct and louder the nearer they got. "It's the general store! What is going on there?" Amy said, pointing to the activity around the building.

"We've only been away a few days. How could it have changed so much in that time? What has Manuel been up to in our absence?"

CHAPTER TWENTY-SEVEN

Josh, who had been driving the buggy that morning, drew up to halt Bella in front of the chaos at the general store. There was timber in one untidy pile, a man up a ladder, and two other men working on the far side of the general store itself.

"Manuel is starting the new extension to the general store," Amy stated the obvious, staring around them at all the confusion. "I wonder if we stable Bella as usual round the back?"

They sat for a moment, and then Manuel rushed round from the back of the building shouting instructions to the men. He caught sight of them both and rushed over, his arms waving excitedly. "I've started it—the saloon is nearly finished and the men building it have come over to start building my hardware store. Come on, round the back. The stables have not been touched. You can put Bella and your buggy in there, as usual. Then come and see what's been happening. There's so much that has changed whilst you were away. You'll see an enormous difference." The stocky little Mexican man rushed off, shouting more instructions at the men. Josh noticed the men listened to him, nodded, then carried on working as before, ignoring his comments and instructions. Manuel just shrugged and rushed back into the store.

"Amy, thank goodness you've arrived! How I've missed you the last few days. So has your goddaughter, little Isabel." Eliza rushed up to Amy and, taking her by her hand, took the girl into the private room where Isabel was sleeping soundly. "She sleeps through all the noise the men make; even all their shouting doesn't disturb her. Last night, when the men finished work and it became quiet, she woke up crying."

After Amy had exclaimed how beautiful Isabel was and how much she had grown, Eliza seemed to relax. "It's been so difficult with all the work going on, coping with Isabel and the customers, but I have been fortunate having Dora, now she's living in here. She has been a marvellous help to me. The hotel is being refurbished now as well as the saloon. Everything is changing in Nowhere. The hotel owner asked Dora to leave the room she was renting permanently from him. So, she has moved in here for now. She is going to be a permanent live-in help to us and will run the hardware side of the store. Dora now has a place to live, and we have permanent staff, so we all benefit."

Before Eliza could tell Amy any more, Manuel called to them. Customers had come in, and he was finding it difficult to cope with them and sort out all the deliveries. The general store was busy that morning. Amy realized that many of the customers had just come in to see what was happening. Nowhere was a small place, and anything unusual caught the attention of the few people who called it home. Josh had been helping Manuel, who greeted his assistance with great enthusiasm and, in no time at all, they were loaded up and set off on the deliveries.

"I left the deliveries until your return, Josh. I heard bandits are wandering about, and there's talk of renegade Indians amongst Devil's Mountain. Having your company and gun along with me seemed a good idea, and Eliza wouldn't hear of me going on my own. What happened out at Dry Creek Ranch?"

The journey to the first property they were delivering to, which was the Grangers', passed quickly as Josh related the story of the bandits at Dry Creek Ranch.

Rosita's declaration that she was leaving the ranch and returning home, and the family's immediate journey back to her home town, was also told to Manuel. Amy and his expedition up into the mountains after the Jesuit gold and their meeting with Sam was not related to Manuel. It was not told to anyone outside Broken Horseshoe Ranch. No one else knew that Luke had arrived with a map and had been searching for the Jesuit gold.

Nowhere was a place where strangers arrived with secrets hidden in their past. Some, like Luke, had reasons that they kept to themselves as to why they had actually come to Nowhere. Others just arrived by chance, running away from something or someone. They stayed and made a life for themselves, but never divulged the real reason they had come to Nowhere.

"I enjoy coming to the Grangers. They not only spend money with me, but they also make us so welcome," Manuel said as he drove the buggy under the large sign which stated in large letters, 'The Grangers'.

"Yes, I hope Mrs Granger has made that delicious coffee cake. I don't think I've ever tasted anything so wonderful," Josh agreed.

They drew up outside the homestead, which was one of the better-quality buildings in the area. The Grangers, unlike many other newcomers to Nowhere, arrived with money and they had built their own home, planned out so that Mrs Granger had a garden. Their property was on a slight rise and looked down at the Avon River. This was one of the few rivers that kept flowing throughout the dry season. This had been essential because Mrs Granger loved growing flowers. In a barren land, water was a treasure that gave life. The plants and flowers that survived in the burning heat and the wild winds that blew across the desert lands were an extravagance, but they made an amazing sight.

"Come on in, come in!" The welcoming smile of Mr Granger, as he ushered them both in, was mirrored by his wife, who was also pleased to see them. Visitors were few; each one, arriving with their news and gossip, was company was to be enjoyed.

Manuel followed them into the kitchen and gave Josh a knowing look as he saw, on the table, a freshly baked coffee cake. The initial greetings over, they sat round the table enjoying a slice of cake with the welcome coffee.

The excitement of Jesse James being seen, the hold-up at Dry Creek Ranch had been discussed, and Manuel's new extension at the general store talked over. It was time for the Grangers to give their news.

"Charles Roberts has brought in two new homesteaders to his plots of land. At the moment they have water—after the rains the creek is full of water flowing down from the mountains. What will happen to them when the creek dries up?" Mr Granger said, spreading out his hands in a despairing gesture.

"Yes, dear, we all know about the lack of water there," Mrs Granger said in an exasperated voice. "Do tell them about that man. He's a terrible man. Go on, tell them all about the prophet!"

CHAPTER TWENTY-EIGHT

Another slice of cake was proffered to both Manuel and Josh by Mrs Granger. Both men accepted eagerly, and she then offered them another cup of coffee.

"Nonsense! They need something stronger than coffee. Here, let's have a glass of whiskey. That'll make the journey back go quicker." A glass of whiskey was poured out in front of each of them. Josh's eyes widened at the height of the whiskey in his glass. Then he looked at his host, who had continued pouring into the top of his glass. Mrs Granger's face showed she was not pleased with the amount of whiskey her husband was consuming. She said nothing, and Josh hoped that their genial host was not turning into a drunk. He liked the man who treated everyone the same and was generous with his wealth. He'd hate to see him go down that path.

"I need this drink, my dear. After my last experience with our new neighbour, it was have a drink of whiskey or shoot the man!" A large slurp from his overflowing glass, and then Mr Granger placed it with a thump on the table. "I'm an easy-going man. I don't take offence or harbour ill will towards any man. Everyone can vouch for that, can't you?" This sudden question barked out at both Manuel and Josh made them jump. They both readily murmured their agreement to his remark. It was true: the man *was* easy-going and pleasant.

Josh wondered what was coming next. He'd never seen the man sitting in front of him so angry yet confused at the same time.

"There's two plots of land been sold. On one is a quiet man who has just settled in with no bother. He came here one day, introduced himself, and pointed out the boundary he'd been told was his and wished to check with me it was correct. Wise man—he wanted to make sure there were no boundary problems with me in the future. Don't like that Charles Roberts: nasty sly man beneath that smarmy manner of his but, got to give him his due, the land has been properly marked out and the deeds are all done by proper lawyer folk."

Another large gulp of the whiskey was swallowed, and then his glass was put down carefully. Mr Granger continued: "But it's this other guy, living on the second plot. He and his wife and son arrived on our doorstep. First words he says to me was whether I was a God-fearing person."

Mrs Granger laughed; her husband scowled at her.

"My dear, it's no laughing matter!"

"You should have seen his face. I've never seen my husband look so thunderstruck and yet at a complete loss for words. The man stood there on our porch, with a large sheaf of Biblical quotation papers in his hands, which he waved about in our faces. A meek little woman stood behind him," said Mrs Granger.

A glare from her husband, and she sat back, allowing him to continue the story—but still she smiled at the memory.

"Did I go to church? Did I read my Bible daily? That's what he asked me first—no pleasant 'Howdy' or introduction. Oh no! Then, and then…" The man paused in his story and reached for his glass. It was empty. "Another whiskey? Josh? Manuel? It's going to be a long, hot dusty journey for you back to Nowhere. Have you got any more deliveries?" he asked both men.

Manuel looked longingly at the whiskey. Josh smiled to himself. The whiskey excelled, a stark contrast to

Nowhere's homemade liquor. Made in sheds or even in tents, the whiskey concocted from homemade stills could be harsh and sometimes lethal!

"Well, Mr Granger, we've a couple more deliveries before we can set out for home," Manuel said, and pushed his glass across the table.

Josh drank little as a rule, but that was a superb whiskey that slid down the tongue and warmed the stomach with a golden glow. His glass was also pushed across the table.

Mrs Granger gave a loud snort, and she watched the whiskey poured into the three glasses: "You'd better have some more cake to mop all that alcohol up!"

"This man stood on my porch. I told you—never even said 'How you do?' or anything about moving into the land adjoining my boundaries. He asked about the preacher and had we got a church in Nowhere. I told him our preacher is also our sheriff. On a Sunday, he has a service in the saloon." Mr Granger took a breath, followed by another slurp of whiskey.

Mrs Granger took up the story: "While the men were talking, I spoke to the wife, and I asked where she was from and how she enjoyed living on their property. Then I asked her if they were building their cabin yet." Mrs Granger sat looking down at that remains of her piece of cake, and played with a couple of crumbs on the plate. "I found her strange indeed. All she would say was 'God led Jeremiah to the desert, and God will provide'. Mr Charles Roberts had brought them in his own carriage to their land. They'd followed him in a wagon, which they were living out of for the moment. I thought she was going to tell me about where they came from, but her husband told her to be quiet. So, I know little about where she came from or why they have arrived here."

Leaning forward, Mr Granger looked at both men and shook his head. "This man told me God had said his name was Jeremiah, and he was a prophet sent out to this land to convert everyone. And he was going to start with us! He told us both to get down on our knees and pray. Shouted at us, in fact, and told us we were sinners and had to get down on our knees and pray at once!" Mr Granger looked at them both to see the expression on their faces. He wasn't disappointed. Both Manuel and Josh were astounded at this.

"What did you do?" Manuel asked Mr Granger.

CHAPTER TWENTY-NINE

"To be honest, I was absolutely amazed," Mrs Granger said, laughing at the memory. "The man who called himself Jeremiah was dressed in dirty blue overalls and had a long white beard with wild, straggly white hair. I've never seen anyone with eyes so staring and angry. He was frightening. I felt sorry for his wife—she stood there in a faded print dress that hung around her thin body, with a huge bonnet that seemed to cover most of her face. All this time, the son sat in the buggy staring at us."

Her husband, determined to get his story out before she could tell it all to Josh and Manuel, interrupted her: "Before I brought my wife inside for our own safety, it was unbelievable what happened. Do you know? Do you know what happened next? That man stood on my porch. On my very own porch! He shouted at me to repent for my sins. When I wouldn't either pray or repent, that man stood there and, putting his face into mine, he called down vengeance on me for not praying. He shouted at me, promising retribution for my sins. All the time he was shouting at me, and the woman stood there singing hymns."

Mr Granger picked up the whiskey glass. To his surprise, it was empty. But a look from his wife was, at this time, enough to deter him from pouring out another glass.

When they left the Grangers', both men were exceedingly happy, and they were full of whiskey and coffee cake. The next two deliveries were speedily dealt with. Almost routine visits, these homesteaders had little to say and didn't want to gossip. Their journey back to Nowhere was spent discussing the strange newcomers.

"I don't know how he'll get on with the preacher. Sheriff Lance Grey is a man who doesn't tolerate fools or interference in how he does his job. He's a good man to have in charge of Nowhere," Manuel said. "He's handy with his gun, he knows his Bible, and he's a pleasant enough man, if a bit intimidating. But no one seems to know anything about him. Where he's come from? What's he doing in Nowhere?" Manuel shook his head. "Best not to worry about it, and definitely not ask the man questions. Might shoot you first before he answers!"

The journey continued, with both men pleasantly mellow, and the heat of the sun was past its hottest and now, in the late afternoon breeze, they felt the worst of the day was over. The weather that day might have been improving, but when they got to Nowhere they realized that Main Street was in an uproar.

"That's Zach the bar tender, fighting—and look, there'se another couple of guys from the saloon joining in. What's going on here, Josh?" Manuel brought the buggy to a halt as the trail from the Grangers ranch turned into Main Street. The road, continuing to the general store, was blocked by fighting men. Shouts and yells could be heard, but it was confusing to the new arrivals as to who were actually fighting whom, and what it was about.

"Look, I can see Amy and Eliza on the boardwalk in front of the general store. They've both got rifles and are pointing them towards the men," Josh said.

"Leave the buggy here. We've got to find out what's going on. Amy and Eliza won't hold off those men for long if they decide to attack the general store. Quick, Josh, let's go!" Manuel flung himself from the buggy and ran towards the general store and the women standing in front of its door. Josh followed him and, being younger and fitter, soon overtook the slower Mexican. Skirting the fighting men, Josh was uncertain which side he should fight on.

"Hey, you! Where do yo think you're going?" Josh had nearly reached the store when his arm was grabbed from behind and a burly man swung around towards him. The man's fist came up, ready to punch Josh on the chin. His arm still in the burly men's grasp, Josh tried to pull away, ducking under that oncoming punch at the same time.

"Josh! Over here! Come and help Zach!" The voice of the saloon owner called to Josh over the hubbub of the fighting men.

The burly man had lost his balance when Josh dodged away from him. Using that advantage, Josh punched the man in the jaw. As the man staggered back, Josh turned and ran towards Zach, who was fighting off two men. Josh rushed up to the aid of the young man, throwing yet another punch at a man who was about to throttle Zach whilst his companion was raining blows down upon the hapless Zach.

Both the opponents Zach and Josh were facing were huge brawny men. Well used to heavy manual work, they had shoulders and arms bulging with muscles. Josh had been happy to go to the aid of his friend but, on summing up their opponents, he did not rate their chances of coming out of this encounter unscathed.

CHAPTER THIRTY

The shots, fired in unison, made every man fighting freeze and turn towards the shooters. To Josh's astonishment, both Eliza and Amy had joined with the sheriff to fire off their guns together. The noise of the women's rifles and the sheriff's guns firing together had been enough for the men to stop fighting and to stand staring at the sheriff.

"Get going before I haul you all off to jail! Get out of my sight and out of my town! Nowhere is a peaceful place, and I aim to keep it that way. Don't come back here if you're going to be fighting and shooting up the place." The tall figure of Sheriff Lance Grey was always imposing but, standing on the boardwalk with a gun in each hand, he looked formidable. His black hat was worn above the long, curling black hair, and the black coat with the long tails that he always wore over his black trousers and shirt added to the dominating presence of the man. Every person on Main Street knew he meant what he said. Fists were dropped, and hands fell to the men's sides as they shuffled their feet and began trooping down the street to their horses. Blood was wiped from bruised and cut faces, and knuckles flexed as fists were opened and closed, trying to relieve the pain brought on by the many punches they had thrown.

The two enormous men—who were about to fight Zach and Josh—gave them both a nod and walked over to their horses standing patiently outside the saloon.

"Thanks for coming to my rescue, Josh," said Zach.

"I don't think I'd have done much good, but at least I came to try," laughed Josh as they both watched the two men climb on their horses and ride away. "Neither of us stood much of a chance against those two," he added.

"Who were they? They were huge men and had large meaty fists."

Zach was still mopping the blood from his lips, which had suffered a heavy blow in the fighting. He gave them a last wipe and answered Josh: "Miners—they came into the saloon and took offence at those other guys who were already drinking in the bar. Don't even know what it was about, but they all started fighting. We were trying to clear them out of the saloon before they wrecked the place. Just got that saloon looking good. We didn't want those roughnecks trashing the place."

"Well, when we came into Nowhere they were all outside fighting, so that worked. You got them out of the saloon," Josh said, and began rubbing his aching chin.

The two men walked over to the general store. Amy and Eliza had dropped their rifles to their sides and, with Sheriff Grey, were still watching the men as they slowly drifted away from the main street of Nowhere.

"That got rid of them, didn't it?" Josh said as he and Zach reached the general store. He looked up at the two women and the sheriff, and smiled at the satisfied looks on their faces.

The aftermath of the large-scale fight that had taken place down Main Street was soon cleared away. The only men left standing were those that had been working in the saloon when the fight broke out. No one was sure of what caused it, just some chance remark that another man, perhaps full of drink, had taken offence to and the first punch was thrown. That was all it took to cause a fight when men came in exhausted, suffering from the heat, and then indulged in alcohol.

The sheriff had remained standing on the boardwalk, his hands very much in evidence: each one poised over his gun holsters. The last weary men rode off, most toward Duloe. They weren't going to that town itself: they would turn off down the trail across the foothills to the silver mine. Halfway between the town, they called Nowhere, and of the much larger town of Duloe lay the silver mine. Most miners opted for the larger town with more going on in it, for there were several saloons, and more businesses had grown up there. Others preferred to come to Nowhere and, when they first started coming, had been made welcome in the saloon. But it was doubtful they would be made welcome again if they continued fighting and breaking up the place.

"What are you going to do about those bars in the jail, Sheriff?" Manuel asked the man outright. "Best get them up in that window, now there are so many fights breaking out in the town, and too many lawbreakers wandering through Nowhere. Don't want them climbing out the window."

The sheriff looked down his long nose at him, and Manuel immediately regretted his question. After a pause, the sheriff spoke: "They're welcome to climb out the window but they'll be dead before they reach the ground!"

The sheriff's words were said in a matter-of-fact tone that struck chills down Josh's back. Everyone within hearing distance stared at the man. There was no doubting his words. That's what Sheriff Lance Grey said, and no one doubted that's what he would do. "Seems peaceful now. I'll be going back to my office. Good day, everyone." The tall, black-clad figure walked with a firm stride up the street to the sheriff's office, leaving silence behind him. "Who is that man? Where did he come from?" The words from Manuel fell into the silence left by the departing sheriff. There was no reply to his questions; no one knew anything about the man. Josh looked at each face around him and could see the same blank expression on every one of them. That expression Josh knew was also on his own. The sheriff was an enigmatic man and no one dared to question him further. What secrets were hidden behind that mask-like face and solemn demeanour?

CHAPTER THIRTY-ONE

It was Eliza who treated Zach and Josh's wounds. They weren't too bad, and both men made light of them. Manuel had rescued the buggy from where they had left it when they arrived in the town and saw the disturbance on Main Street. Coffee laced with whiskey was poured out for Josh and Zach by Manuel, who felt that it was desperately needed after the fight.

"I'll not refuse this—but I've never drank so much whiskey in a single day," said Josh.

Amy had gone back to her small table and was bending over the ledger, finishing the accounts for Manuel. At this remark, she looked up, put the pen down, and turned towards him. "Where else were you drinking whiskey today?"

Eliza came in to the store and sat down on a chair to nurse Isabel, who was sleepy after feeding. "What's this all about? Who gave you whiskey, and why?"

Manuel was leaning against the counter in the general store, a mug of whiskey-laced coffee in his hand. "It was at the Grangers' place. The first two plots to be sold by Charles Roberts have got their new owners. One man has moved in and Mr Granger says he is polite and wanted to double check his boundaries with him, which put him in Mr Granger's good books immediately. But it's the other couple and their son: they came to the Grangers' place demanding that they repent of their sins and pray with them. The man says he is the prophet Jeremiah and has been sent to Nowhere to do God's work."

Manuel's audience had increased. Dora, holding a broom and sweeping up the boardwalk, stood staring open-mouthed at Manuel. Another couple of ladies—who had taken refuge in the store whilst the fighting men had been outside and had remained to finish their shopping—now stood excitedly listening to this latest gossip about the newcomers to Nowhere.

The spittoon placed in front of the counter gave a loud ding and thump as the chew of tobacco landed in it. All eyes looked at Dora, who had finished chewing, and always spat it out, achieving her aim no matter how far she was away from the spittoon. Josh disliked seeing her chew tobacco but was always impressed by the skill she showed in aiming for that spittoon. Dora drew in a large breath and shook her head. "Sheriff Grey won't take too kindly to being told to repent his sins by this so-called prophet. No, he won't like it at all! I only hope I'm there to watch what he does when he meets this man called Jeremiah!"

Isabel was asleep, so Eliza joined Amy for a chat before Amy and Josh set off home to Broken Horseshoe Ranch. The two women were standing talking as Amy tidied away the paperwork she had been working on that day. "I've nearly finished the accounts. It can only be a short time tomorrow and they will be done." Closing the books and setting them neatly on one side of the table, Amy was pleased that she had done this task. She was useful still in the general store. Now, with Dora arriving and living in the new hardware store, and helping every day, Amy was worried that her position at the general store would disappear. Josh was indispensable. In fact, with the new people moving into the area, his help was even more necessary for Manuel, both in his deliveries and in the heavy work in the new hardware store.

"These vegetables won't last much longer. Take some back home with you, Amy," Eliza said, putting vegetables into a bag. As she did so, the door opened and two men walked into the store. Amy recognized them both immediately—and she knew Eliza had also remembered them. Eliza had frozen. Her hands on the bruised vegetables had begun to shake. They were part of the group of men that had bought up most of the provisions in the store earlier that week.

Amy walked over and smiled at them. "Can I help you?" she said politely.

One reached into his vest pocket and pulled out a scribbled note. He pushed it towards her across the counter. "Everything on that list, or the nearest to it. We'll be back for it after we've been to the saloon." He turned on his heel and walked out the door, his companion following him. The voice of the man behind drifted back towards the women. "Don't you get drunk. You know what Jesse said about drinking? Don't want to get him mad at you. He's pretty quick on the draw, remember?"

Eliza rushed over to look down at the list. "What do we do? That's those two men who were in that group who gave us all that money. He spoke of Jesse when he went out the door. They must be in Jesse James's gang. Amy, what do we do?"

CHAPTER THIRTY-TWO

"We'll get this list ready for them on their return. That's what we'll do, Eliza. I'll start the list. You go next door and tell Josh and Manuel. One of them can tell the sheriff. Or should we just finish up the order they're asking for and not bother telling the men? We don't want a shootout in the store, do we?"

Whilst Amy was talking quietly, she was busy getting all the items from the list the man had left on the counter. There were the usual provisions that every man travelling throughout the West required: she piled up the sacks of beans, coffee, and flour on one side. Eliza, hesitant at first, began moving quickly to help Amy fill out the list, and reached for a couple of empty sacks in which to put the goods.

"I'll help you first. Can't leave you alone in here. If I'm not here when they return, it will look suspicious," Eliza said, thinking things through despite her fear of the bandits.

"Thank goodness you stayed," whispered Amy, when the men returned in a very short time. They could have only had one drink, she thought. Neither wanted to go against Jesse James's orders. One drink would be acceptable by the bandit after a journey through the heat of the day in desert lands.

"There's everything on your list. We've put them in these two sacks for you." Amy put the list on top of the sacks and pushed them across the counter towards the men.

Both looked round the store, checking to see if the store was still empty, before coming to the counter. "I'll have a couple of these," one man said, bringing over a couple of cans of condensed milk to add to the sack.

Reaching into the pocket of the dusty jacket he wore, the man pulled out a small pouch. It jingled as he held it in his hand. Without opening it, or even looking at it, he handed it to Eliza. "Thanks," he said and picked up one sack. The other man picked up the other one, gave a nod to both women, and both went out of the store. Amy and Eliza watched as the men put the sacks into a buggy and drove away.

"I'll get Manuel," Eliza said and rushed off through the back door of the general store and round to the new building— that was going to be the hardware store— taking place. "Manuel! Manuel!" Eliza's voice could be heard over the noise of the banging and hammering. All noise ceased, and Amy knew they were listening to Eliza. Her attention turned to the small bag on the counter. It was a small leather pouch with a drawstring closing it. Amy worked at the drawstring, pulling it open and emptying its contents. Coins fell in a steady stream onto the counter. As they landed, they jostled each other, clinking together in a pile. Amy could only stare down at the mixture of coinage, but it was the two gold coins that caught her attention.

"Whoever these men were, wherever they had come from, they certainly had money with them," Amy whispered into the empty general store.

Footsteps clattered up the stairs. The back door of the general store was flung open and Josh raced in, followed by Manuel and Eliza.

"Amy! Are you all right? You're certain it was the James gang?" Josh's words came out in a rush and she can see by the anxious expression on his face how much cared for her.

"Look at the payment you've got for those goods, Eliza!" Amy pointed down at the pile of coins.

"They handed us a pouch, we didn't know what was in it, if anything," said Eliza. "I only hoped there was money in it—but we weren't going to argue with them, were we, Amy?" Eliza's colour was coming back after the fear she had sustained at the arrival of the bandits.

Amy was relieved to see that Eliza could even joke again. Amy herself was feeling decidedly wobbly. Those men had been frightening. There was an overpowering aura of evil about them. Amy had feared them. There was a callous indifference in the way they looked at the women. She had felt certain that they would shoot both Eliza and her and think no more of it, as if they were swatting a fly. Their eyes had been cold, hard, and without emotion. All she could do was sit down quickly and be thankful that both she and Eliza had survived.

CHAPTER THIRTY-THREE

"Don't forget your vegetables," Eliza said to Amy. Josh had helped Manuel clear up in the new shop next door for the night. He had arrived back in the general store itself to get ready for their return to Broken Horseshoe Ranch.

Amy's bag was ready on the small accounts table she now used. She was shrugging her jacket on, and took the sack of vegetables from Eliza, placing it on the small table beside her bag.

"What a day! You'll have plenty to tell them at the ranch when you get home," said Eliza.

Amy gave her friend a sympathetic smile and agreed that it had been quite a day. Dora, who had been helping organize the hardware delivery next door (that had arrived earlier with the carrier for Manuel), had also followed Josh into the store.

"What a long day it's been. Thank goodness that's over. You've only got your journey home and then you can rest up," Manuel said. He walked over to the door and was about to lock it for the night when it was thrust open. Manuel stepped hurriedly back as three men marched into the store. Following them came Sheriff Grey with a worried look on his face.

"Who served those men who've just been in here?" the sheriff demanded.

Nervous looks towards Amy and Eliza were sent by Manuel, but it was Amy who stepped forward and opened her mouth to speak. She didn't have a chance to answer him.

The sheriff was pushed to one side. "I'll handle this, Sheriff. No need for you to be involved," said the largest of the men, walking further into the store and standing before the two women.

Josh was aware of the sheriff's displeasure at the arrival of these men. He watched as the sheriff stood back. He had a grim look on his face as the three men swaggered around the store. What were they, Josh wondered? Who were they? They looked as if they had authority and power, which they were not afraid to use. All three men were dressed in black coats, trousers, and boots, not unlike Sheriff Grey's outfit. But somehow, on these men, it was a uniform—and was threatening on all three.

"Have a look at these drawings. Can you tell me if any of these were the men who came into the store and bought provisions from you?" Several papers with drawings on them were spread on the counter. Amy and Eliza stared down at them.

It was Eliza who pointed to one and looked at Amy: "Isn't that the one who bought everything and spoke to us, Amy? I think it was him, wasn't it?"

Amy nodded, flicked through some more papers, and pointed at another drawing. "And that's the second man, isn't it, Eliza?" As Amy came to the last paper, she picked it up and held it out to Josh. "Josh, that's the man we buried. That man had those special papers on him."

The large, burly man looked down at the paper with the drawing on it. His jaw tightened, and his face took on an even grimmer expression than the one he was already wearing. He looked at those gathered in the general store. "Out, all of you! Now! Only you two stay behind." He gestured to Josh and Amy.

"But I'm the sheriff of Nowhere." Sheriff Grey began to speak.

But the man turned to face him and put one hand on

his pistol in its holster and hissed one word: "Out!"

Sheriff Grey, with a despairing look at Josh and Amy, left. Manuel and the others had also retreated into the back room. Josh moved closer to Amy and put his arm around her shoulder. He wondered if he was giving her moral support—or was he gaining support for himself? This man was powerful and frightening. What was he going to do with them?

"What happened to the man?"

"He was hiding behind bushes, about to kill an Apache family: a man, a woman, and a young boy. We killed him and buried the body." Josh's arm tightened on Amy's shoulder. How he hoped she wouldn't speak. He hoped his explanation would keep this man happy.

"How did you kill him?" came the next question.

Again, Josh's grip tightened on Amy's shoulder, a signal that she should keep quiet. How he hoped she would contradict nothing he said or add to it. "I threw a knife into his back. It killed him outright."

Amy moved slightly at this remark from Josh, but she didn't add to his story or say anything.

"Did you read all the papers?" Again, the question came—this time with an intent, probing look on the man's face.

"No, we saw they were important documents and just left them in the packet they came in, then handed it to Sheriff Gray." Josh's answers seem to be satisfactory, because the man just nodded his head.

"You never saw that man. You didn't kill him or bury his body. Those papers were never in your possession. Is that understood?" An icy stare transfixed both of them, awaiting their reply.

"Yes," said Amy.

"Yes," Josh said and added, "We understand that we never saw the man or his papers."

"Remember: if you speak of this, not only you will die, but every member of your family will suffer the same fate." Another hard, sharp look at both of them, and he turned on his heel and walked out of the door.

CHAPTER THIRTY-FOUR

"What did that man want? Are you both all right?" Sheriff Grey came in as the men walked along the boardwalk to stand talking together beside their horses.

"Yes, everything's fine. There was no problem. He just thought we'd seen something that might help him look for Jesse James," said Josh.

"Yes, that's right. There was no problem at all," echoed Amy.

The suspicious look that spread over Sheriff Grey's face showed he didn't believe a word of it. But he glanced out of the window at the men standing there, and decided it was better for all concerned that he didn't ask any more questions.

An uproar at the top of Main Street was coming closer, and Sheriff Grey rushed out of the door to see what was going on. Josh yelled for Manuel and the others to come and see what was happening. That way, they would forget to ask about the man and his need for a secret conversation.

"We got these two members of the gang—we caught up with them along the trail!" A group of six men, escorting the two men in the buggy, drew up in front of the group of three government men.

"Where's Jesse James? You better tell us. That way you may live." Again, it was the tall, burly man who took charge, stepping forward to question the two men sitting in the buggy.

"He's gone. Left two days ago to head up north. He's heard that a gold shipment is going to be easy pickings. He's gone to hold up ..." began one man in the buggy.

"Why are you still here? And what are you doing

staying in Devil's Mountain?" The men looked at each other, then looked back at the tall man, who pulled out his gun. He shot one man in the arm and gave a slow, calculating smile. "I have plenty more bullets, but you don't have many more limbs. Tell me now, and you might live."

Clutching his arm, trying to stem the blood that was flowing freely down onto his wrist and hand, the man wailed at him. "We've got a hideout up at Bandits' Butte. We stay there and keep guard of the area. Jesse James has hidden money up in Lonesome Creek canyon. We don't know where he's hidden it, but we have to kill anyone who looks as if they're digging for his hidden gold. That's all we're doing. We never took part in any robberies. We just met him when he rode into Duloe. Honest, we're not bank robbers. We were just paid to mind Lonesome Creek canyon."

The tall man turned to his two companions. "Do you believe him? He looks stupid, only fit enough to guard the canyon. I think we take them with us."

"You reckon Jesse James has gone? That the man is telling the truth?" said one of the men in black.

The tall man turned back to the buggy. "If you don't want me to shoot a hole in the other arm, tell me the truth. Where is Jesse James?"

The wounded man whimpered at the gun that was waved at his healthy arm. "It's the truth, Jesse James left two days ago. Ask the women—we've just bought enough food for the two of us. Only two of us, not for the entire gang. They left. Honest, it's the truth."

"Take them both and put them in the cell," the man said. "We'll stay the night in the hotel and then leave early in the morning. Nothing to stay here for. You men, go and camp outside town. And no drinking in the saloon. Early start in the morning."

With that, he and his two companions climbed on their horses. As he turned to ride away, he gave one last look at Josh and Amy and nodded his head at them. Both felt the chills run down their spines at that intent warning look.

It was a long journey in the dark back to Broken Horseshoe Ranch. Neither Josh nor Amy felt like talking. The day had been long too long, and they were both worn out. So much seemed to have happened in the last few days that they felt breathless at the speed of how fast everything had occurred. Met by the family as usual, and with David clinging to Amy, they ate their meal almost falling asleep over it.

Josh told the story in its barest terms, his words stumbling over each other with the fatigue he was being overwhelmed by. Thankfully, Luke and the others realized their exhaustion and left them alone with not one question asked, despite their intense curiosity.

Next morning, the questions flowed thick and fast, and both Josh and Amy felt able to answer them. But they did not mention the Confederate papers, or the man who had ordered their silence on the pain of death to themselves and their loved ones. They set off for the general store at the usual time, still tired, and still trying to process the events of the last few days.

Amy, listening to Josh tell of how many deliveries he was expecting to help Manuel with that day, could only wonder if her time at the general store would be over soon. With Dora living on the premises, it seemed that the three of them serving and helping in the general store was one person too many. Amy was dreading to be told that she was no longer needed. The money, or rather the exchange for the labour of herself for goods and provisions, had made a big difference to their life at Broken Horseshoe Ranch. But it wasn't only that which concerned Amy: it was the friendship she had with Eliza that was so precious—she didn't want to lose it. Having no sister, and losing her mother before moving to Nowhere, Eliza, who was closer to her in age than Nancy, was a friend and confidante.

Amy didn't burden Josh with these concerns of hers. Perhaps something would work out, she thought.

CHAPTER THIRTY-FIVE

Bella was stabled, and Josh wandered in after Amy to the general store. Manuel had some of the delivery boxes already packed and had only another couple to do. Josh greeted Eliza and was fingering some of the new deliveries of flannel shirts when Charles Roberts walked into the store.

As usual, his eyes lit up when he saw Amy, and his good manners towards Eliza and Manuel always won them over to his charm. Josh was surprised and pleased to see how Amy kept a polite distance from the man without being rude to him.

"I've some new people moving into Nowhere—a wonderful old man with his wife and son. He styles himself as a prophet and says the Lord has brought him to Nowhere to convert the people of the area into the Way."

"What Way?" Josh asked Charles, looking at the man suspiciously.

"I don't know what Way, but when I told him about the preacher and the services held each Sunday in the saloon, he was pretty angry. I foresee some interesting conversations between him and the preacher in the future. There are two other gentlemen taking up residence in the lots I have sold. Both single men, trying to carve out a living and life here in Nowhere. Of course, Manuel, I have told them all about your wonderful store." Charles gave a slight bow to Manuel and Eliza as he delivered these flowery words.

He picked up the few provisions he was buying, paid Eliza, gave Amy a charming farewell speech, and then turned to walk past Josh.

"Josh Barnes, I think you've had a very pleasant, quiet

time lately. I do hope you enjoyed it—because that has ended. In fact, life is going to be lively for you soon. Watch your back!" He had a sneering smile at the surprised look on both Josh and Amy's faces, and he went out of the door.

"What did he mean?" Amy had come up beside Josh, as both of them watched Charles Roberts strut down Main Street. He raised a hand in greeting to everyone he met, shouted remarks to the men across the street, and lifted his hat and bowed low to every woman he saw. Josh noticed everyone smiled back at him. The women turned and watched his progress with approving smiles on their faces.

"My would-be killer has obviously been in touch with him, and I'm about to be targeted yet again," Josh said. "If only I could remember my past! Losing my memory means that I am at a loss as to knowing who could want to kill me. Why do they want me dead?"

"There's nothing we can do, is there?" Amy asked him, putting her hand on his arm. "We must take care Josh and watch out for any strangers and be prepared for any unforeseen occurrence."

Pushing his hair back from his face, Josh smiled down at the girl beside him, his eyes crinkling with amusement and tenderness. *Amy had said we must take care.* That meant so much to him. He wasn't alone in this situation. He tried not to smile at her face, but she had pursed her lips and drawn her brows down in a ferocious frown. It didn't quite work, because those freckles and her sparkling eyes could never become an evil expression. Not that Amy couldn't act, and even kill a man, but no matter what she did, she still had that aura of goodness around her.

Work continued in the general store. The last of the delivery orders were packed and ready to go into the wagon. Amy had finished the accounts, and was standing beside Dora and Eliza, looking very concerned. They only had a few customers that morning, and each one of them had rushed to serve the person.

Manuel came up to Amy carrying a large cardboard box. The sheepish expression on his face warned her he was not bringing good news. Was this a farewell gift for her?

"Amy, I told everyone that you are doing my accounts, and you made a good job of them." Manuel stopped speaking and looked at his wife. Eliza gave a nod of her head and he continued. "With Dora now living and working in the hardware store, Eliza has help all day now. But Seth at the saloon, and the new hotel owner, have all asked me to approach you and ..."

Eliza pushed her husband aside. Grabbing the box from him, she put it in Amy's hands. "Both the saloon and the hotel need their accounts doing. I don't want to lose you coming here, so I agreed you could do the accounts for their businesses at your usual table here in the store."

Amy put the box of papers on the table and smiled. Maybe doing accounts wouldn't be too bad after all.

The door swung open and the imposing figure of a white-haired, white bearded man strode in. He was followed by a mousy woman wearing an oversized bonnet, and a sullen -looking son. The man stood there looking round at the store, and then at each one of them.

"I am the prophet Jeremiah. I have come to this town to rid it of evil. Get down on your knees and pray! Every one of you must repent your sins." His voice was loud and echoed around the general store. Each one of them was transfixed by this man and his hectoring domineering manner. They all stood staring at him.

"Down on your knees! Repent! For you are all damned!"

Boom! The noise of an explosion shattered the quiet Monday morning. The wooden building of the general store shook, dust drifting down from between the roof timbers. Crashing debris could be heard in the yard behind the general store.

"What's happened?" Manuel, dropped the sack of beans he was carrying. "That's an explosion! And it's out in the stable yard." Ignoring the beans which had scattered and rolled all over the floor, he ran towards the back door.

"Josh!" Amy screamed and began running across the wooden floor of the general store. She had been working at a small table at the back of the general store, doing the accounts of the general store and saloon in Nowhere. Amy's fingers were ink-stained, and she flung back the long brown hair that carried the hint of auburn highlights that hung over her shoulders, two long braids, both tied back with the usual twine. Her freckled face and sparkling eyes, usually alight with mischief, were now filled with apprehension and worry. "Josh has just gone out the back door. He was going to saddle up the buggy, ready for our return home to the ranch."

She ran to the back door leading to the stable yard from where the loud explosive noise had originated. Not far behind Amy, Eliza grabbed her skirt, lifting it up, the better to run with. Manuel and Eliza owned and ran the general store. He was a small man, carrying far too much weight, and had large canvas trousers straining at his ample belly, whilst the suspenders strained mightily to keep those enormous trousers up.

The back door of the general store was stuck fast with

the force of the blast that had hit it. It was Amy who reached it first, and she struggled hard to push it open.

"I can't get it! It won't open!" Amy pushed hard again. Nothing happened.

"Move aside, Amy." Amy stepped back, letting Manuel attack the door. Manuel's heavy bulk behind his shoulder made the door fly open with a screeching and groaning sound.

"Josh! Josh, you're hurt!" Amy ran down the steps, both hands lifting her skirt up as she jumped the last two steps to run to the side of the fallen man.

"Josh, speak to me." She fell to her knees beside him. Josh had fallen a short distance away from the steps. He was stirring, and to Amy's eyes seemed unhurt. "Are you hurt? Can you move your limbs?" Her hands ran over his arms and down his ankles.

The tall, muscular man lay sprawled in the dirt. His floppy blond hair was pushed back by his shaking hand as he struggled to rise to his feet. Josh finally stood up and brushed the dirt from his denim trousers, his long, lean legs showing no hurt from the blast that had flung him backwards.

"What happened? I was just walking towards the buggy when I was flung back. Don't fuss Amy. I'm all right. As you can see, I can move everything. My ears are ringing and I feel dizzy. That's all. I'm fine."

"Your buggy! What has happened here? It's been destroyed" Manuel stood beside the two figures of Amy and Josh, his eyes riveted upon a pile of broken and scorched timber that lay scattered around the stable yard. The smoke and smell lingered in the air, whilst the charred remnants of the buggy had crumpled and fallen into ash.

Eliza, reaching them, rushed towards Josh. She began checking Josh over, ignoring his protestations. Realising that Josh was unhurt—just stunned, and only knocked over by the blast—Eliza looked around in horror at the scene of devastation.

"Bella? Oh, no! Has she been hurt?" Amy's voice held almost as much distress for her horse as it had done for Josh. Across the yard in a far corner stood an old adobe building that housed the horses. Manuel's sturdy horse-of-all-work was joined, on the days Josh and Amy helped at the general store, by Bella, the horse belonging to Broken Horseshoe Ranch. Earlier that morning Josh had stabled Bella in the old adobe building as usual, and he usually left the buggy outside the door of the stable. But knowing that they had to pick up provisions that night for the Broken Horseshoe Ranch, he had left the buggy nearer to the general store.

"The buggy! Look at our buggy. It's been destroyed. What happened to the stable? What happened to the horses?" Amy asked in horror, putting both hands to her face. "What's happened to Bella?"

CHAPTER THIRTY-SEVEN

Manuel, could only look around his normally tidy and neat stable yard in dismay. Now, the stable yard was a scene of devastation.

The general store itself was built on higher ground, with wooden steps leading down to the large dirt yard from the back door of the store. Usually, Manual kept the delivery wagon nearer to the store itself, standing beneath the steps. That was handier to carry the delivery boxes down the steps and place the boxes in it. Today, however, was not a delivery day, and the wagon had been kept in the adobe stable.

It was the buggy from Broken Horseshoe Ranch that had been placed near to the steps, ready for those provisions Amy was taking back with her when they had finished work. And it was the buggy that had taken the full force of the blast.

"Why did the buggy explode? How could it happen?" Eliza stood there, staring at the smouldering pile of ash and broken spars of wood. "What did you have in the buggy, Josh? Was there anything in there that could have ..." Eliza's voice faded away as she realized she didn't know what she was saying. After the blast, and she had checked that Josh was all right, Eliza had rushed to the back room where baby Isabel, had been lying asleep.

Isabel had been woken up by the noise, but the baby was unharmed. Eliza had followed the others down the steps into the yard. A small woman, her black hair tied back in a tight bun, Eliza was tough and capable. Growing up in a small Mexican town, she and husband Manuel had sought to better themselves. Eliza, like the others, was shocked by the destruction they had found in the stable yard. Nursing the baby, she stood there looking around.

Manuel had taken one look at the destruction of the buggy and then ran around the broken spars of wood and debris and rushed towards the adobe stable. Supposedly a tough man, Manuel loved his old horse and would have hated to see him hurt. He had brought the horse with them when they had moved from their hometown to Nowhere. The horse had brought them and all their possessions as they embarked on their new venture of running the general store. The previous owner, had built the general store and opened it with optimism by him and his wife. But his wife, originally from back east, disliked frontier living. She hated the desert winds that blew dust everywhere. The insects, the snakes, the spiky cacti, the vegetation: all were sent especially to annoy her. The few settlers that had moved into the area, and were building properties in the town of Nowhere itself, were not to her liking. So, the general store was sold at a bargain price to Eliza and Manuel, who took it over and made a success of it.

"The stable seems undamaged, Amy! I think the animals are safe." His shouts echoed around the stable yard as despite his heavy weight he reached the stable at an amazing pace. "They're safe and unhurt. Come and see, Amy. Our horses are fine."

Amy rushed after Manuel and entered under the low roof of the adobe building behind him. In the cool darkness, they could see both horses were looking shaken. Manuel had his arm around the horse and was patting and, murmuring softly to her. The Spanish endearments were unknown to Amy, but the horse seemed to enjoy them and nuzzled her master.

Bella turned her head around to stare at Amy, and she was delighted to see her horse was unhurt. "Hello, Bella! Thank goodness you're safe." Amy rushed over to the horse, murmuring to her. Across the horse's neck, her eyes met those of Manuel. They both smiled. Their love for their horses was shared between them. The smell of the stable with the hay, and scent of the horses themselves, was a welcome relief from the acrid smoke and explosive residue that was lingering in the air outside.

"Thank goodness the blast didn't reach them. These adobe walls are stronger than they look. But they must have been frightened by the noise," said Amy. The girl was shaking after the shock of the blast. Adding to this shock had been the overwhelming fear of Josh and Bella being hurt, or even killed. Amy loved her horse. Bella had been part of the deal when Luke, her father, had bought Broken Horseshoe Ranch. Somehow, the older horse and the raw eastern girl—a novice to the harsh land, life on the ranch, and even the horses themselves—had bonded. Amy calmed down as she patted the horse, hiding her face away from Manuel so that he did not see the expression she knew would betray her. That moment, when she saw Josh lying immobile and sprawled on the dirt in the stable yard, had brought home to her the depth of her feeling for him. No longer could she deny it. Josh was becoming far more than just a friend.

Amy fought that feeling and pushed it away into the back of her mind. How could she follow her heart and declare her love for Josh? A man with no memory could not embark on a new, lasting relationship. For all they knew, Josh could have a wife and children waiting anxiously for news of him. If Josh regained his memory, and there was neither a wife nor a girlfriend in his past, then—and only then—could they declare their love for each other.

"Oh, no! Manuel, Manuel!" Harsh screams from Eliza echoed round the yard. Manuel spun round and raced out of the adobe stable again, with a speed that amazed Amy, who followed him.

They both came to a sudden halt as their eyes followed the pointing finger of Eliza, who was transfixed in horror. Her mouth was wide open, ready for another piercing scream.

CHAPTER THIRTY-EIGHT

"Inside! Both of you, inside! Eliza, take that baby into the store. This is no place for women." The bellow from Manuel, standing beside her at the entrance to the stable, made Amy jump. Blindly, she ran to Eliza's side and, putting an arm around the shuddering woman, she helped Eliza and the baby towards the steps at the back of the general store.

As she did so, Sheriff Lance Grey swooped around the corner at a run towards them. Coat tails flying behind him, the sheriff's long figure was dressed as usual in a black shirt and vest, and his exceptionally long coat. "What's happened here?" he shouted. A few onlookers, eager to see what caused the explosion they heard, had followed him into the stable yard.

Amy ignored the crowd that was gathering at the entrance to the stable yard and rushed Eliza and Isabel back up the steps into the general store. Both were taken aback to find the store already crowded, and a frantic Dora trying to serve everyone.

Amy looked at Eliza, who was still white-faced and shaking. "Go with Isabel—you see to the baby, and I'll help Dora." Amy gave the woman a gentle shove towards the owner's bedroom. Then she rushed to Dora's side. The older woman gave her a grateful smile as she continued serving.

It didn't take long for Amy to realize that most of the women and men queueing to be served had only come in to find out what was going on. They didn't mind waiting. It gave them more time to gossip about this latest dramatic happening. It didn't matter to Amy; it only increased Manuel's profits at the end of the day, so she smiled at everyone she served.

"I don't know what happened. There seems to have been an explosion in the backyard. No major damage, only the buggy from Broken Horseshoe Ranch in the blast was destroyed." Her voice fell into the silence that had swept over the crowd after she and Eliza had entered the general store.

"That's all I know." Amy held up her hands, to stop the people firing questions at her. "Sheriff Lance Grey is there now. He'll be able to tell you all about it, and what exactly has happened." The murmur of voices showed that, far from satisfying the people milling around the general store, Amy had only whetted their appetite. They wanted more information.

As Dora turned to the back of the counter to measure out items for one customer, Amy joined her, reaching up to a top shelf for a can of condensed milk. "Is that all you saw?" Dora whispered to the girl. "Eliza looks terrible. I heard her screaming as well. What happened out there?" Dora's black bombazine dress rustled as she moved closer to Amy, whispering under her breath so that the customers crowding round the counter couldn't hear. "Eliza doesn't get upset easily. She was obviously shocked. What was it, Amy?"

"I'll tell you later, but not now," Amy said, also under her breath. She turned back with a smile on her face to the customer, holding out the condensed milk for him.

The general store was finally empty. The realization that Amy knew nothing, and was telling them nothing, had emptied the store. Dora wiped her brow before reaching for the tobacco she chewed endlessly. "Now we're alone, you can tell me," she said as she began chewing.

Averting her eyes from that incessant chewing of Dora's, which somehow made her feel queasy, Amy told Dora all about the scene of carnage in the stable yard.

They were joined by Eliza, who was looking brighter: the green tinge had disappeared from her face. "Isabel has gone to sleep. Did you tell Dora about the dead body?" Eliza said. "Who could it be? And why would somebody be in a stable yard with dynamite?" Eliza continued speaking, her thoughts echoing Amy's.

A sick feeling washed over Amy as she realized the truth. The words Charles Roberts had spoken to her and Josh the previous day came into her mind. He had warned Josh that the unknown stalker and killer—who had previously tried to kill Josh—would send more assassins. "Watch your back!" Charles Roberts had called out those last words to Josh as he left the general store.

"I'm certain that it was another killer. It was another attempt to kill Josh. Someone must have been lying in wait, with dynamite to blow him up," Amy said.

Dora's words broke the silence that followed Amy's remarks. The older woman spat out her chew of tobacco into the spittoon. She waited to make sure that she had achieved her aim, nodded at the noise it made when she had been successful, and then she spoke: "Someone is getting desperate. He doesn't care who else he kills in his determination to seek the death of Josh. Why does he want Josh dead? That is important and if he knew maybe Josh could solve the problem."

Dora spread her black skirts and perched on a chair, her dark eyes deep in thought as she puzzled over this conundrum. New to the township of Nowhere, she had been living in the hotel since her arrival. Dora called herself Mrs, but there had been no sign of a husband or mention of one. Obviously a God-fearing woman, she attended the service in the saloon every Sunday. Dora wore her hair straight back in a bun on the back of her neck. Always dressed in black, she favoured the rustling bombazine fabric of the past years. Despite her age, she was strong and always willing to help in the general store. Dora never spoke about her past. This was Nowhere—a collection of makeshift buildings and tent businesses out west. Anyone who arrived here did not need to speak about their past. And no one would ever ask them. That was the unwritten law.

Dora continued voicing her thoughts: "Why is he now so desperate to kill Josh? He wants Josh dead so badly he doesn't care who else he kills. Now anyone close to Josh is also in danger!"

CHAPTER THIRTY-NINE

Heavy feet clumped up the wooden steps into the back of the general store. The three women turned as Manuel and Josh came in. Their faces were grim, and neither spoke.

"Whiskey, Josh?" Manuel didn't wait for Josh's reply but went into the back room and reappeared shortly with the whiskey bottle and two glasses. "I've put on a pot of fresh coffee for you ladies. I can add some whiskey to each cup. You may need it after I tell you what's happened."

Eliza moved closer to Amy and gripped her hand tightly. Dora, still sitting on the stool, took a deep breath and waited for Manuel's announcement.

A large gulp of the whiskey was followed by Manuel taking a deep breath. "Someone was trying to fix dynamite beneath the buggy belonging to the Broken Horseshoe Ranch. It's hot as hell today, and he obviously didn't know what he was doing. We think the dynamite became unstable and exploded as he was trying to fix a fuse." The rest of the whiskey was downed and Manuel reached again for the bottle.

Dora rose to her feet. She walked into the back room after patting Eliza on the shoulder. "Go on, Eliza, sit down. I'll get the coffee for us ladies." The sympathetic glance she gave to the younger woman was noticed by Amy. "Eliza saw the charred body, not an everyday sight or occurrence," Dora said. "Did you see it, Amy?"

At Amy's nod and screwed-up face (at her remembrance of the gruesome sight), Dora looked at her. "But you, Amy, are made of much sterner stuff, my girl. There's not much can disturb your peace. You're going to be a true frontierswoman!"

Amy wasn't too sure about that. Why did Eliza get all the sympathy? Before she could think even more about it, they were conscious of the movement and shouting outside in the main street. Sheriff Grey was shouting instructions to a couple of men who were wheeling a large cart with a tarpaulin over it. No one needed telling. That was the remains of the would-be assassin.

Josh started walking up and down the store. His nervous gestures and agitated steps showed how worried he was. "I'll leave Nowhere. It's no good me staying around. I'm just bringing you all into danger. If that man had been successful, both Amy and I would have been blown up. It could also have been with any of you standing beside us. I'm bringing danger into all your lives." Josh blurted out all these words in a rush, and then swallowed the whiskey from the glass he was holding in one go.

"Seems to me, Josh, we're all in danger living here in Nowhere. Amy and Eliza got involved with those two gangsters the other day, just serving them in the shop. The man who blew himself up is an isolated incident. I see no need for you to hide away or leave Nowhere," Manuel said, his hand reaching out again for the whiskey bottle.

Before he could pour out another glass, Eliza got up and took it into the back room. She could be heard opening cupboard doors before returning to the store. She had her gun in one hand and Manuel's gun in the other. "Instead of reaching for the whiskey bottle, Manuel, strap on your gun. That will be more use to us if we have to face down any more bandits and killers."

Manuel looked at his wife, and licked his lips, thinking sadly of the whiskey bottle now back in the cupboard. But he took the gun from her, strapping on the holster and inspecting the gun thoroughly, he placed it ready on his hip. "Did you have whiskey in that coffee, Eliza? You're suddenly ..." Words failed Manuel as he looked up at his wife.

Eliza put her hands on her hips and glared at him. "I am mad, angry, and determined that Josh should not be run out of town! That evil man got what he deserved. He intended other people to be blown up and become charred bodies. But he became the one who was carted off in bits." The angry vehemence coming from the small Mexican woman made them all stare at her. Only moments ago, she had been shuddering at the sight of the body in the blast. It seemed such a sudden change, and none of them could understand what had happened to Eliza in such a short time.

Seeing their puzzled faces, Eliza explained to them. "Yes, I was upset and horrified. I've never seen such a sight before, I hope I don't see another one like that. But when Josh said he'd better move away to save us, to protect us from his would-be killer, it made me mad. Josh is a *good* man. Since his accident, he's done nothing but help everyone he can. Why should he leave Nowhere? Why should he be forced out by some anonymous cowardly killer? The man hasn't got the guts himself to come and face Josh. Oh, no! He has to send people to do his dirty business. Well ..." Here Eliza tapped the gun which she had placed into her pocket in the voluminous skirts she always wore. "Well, I'm going to be ready for the next one, and I'm going to shoot the varmint!

CHAPTER FORTY

The journey home to Broken Horseshoe Ranch was accomplished by Amy riding Bella and Josh on a horse borrowed from the livery stable. The problem of the buggy replacement was something that would have to be talked over with Luke and Nancy.

Neither of them spoke much as they rode the familiar trail. Because of the explosion, and the delay in sorting themselves out in the aftermath, they were much later than usual. The sun was sinking fast behind the lofty peaks of Devil's Mountain. The hot wind that often blew across the land during the day had dropped. That night, the air seemed heavy as the smell of the vegetation grew stronger and a slight breeze whispered amongst the rocks, vegetation, and cacti.

"I'm sorry, Amy." The apology from Josh jolted Amy from the reverie in which she was riding.

"Sorry for what?" Puzzled by his remark, she glanced sideways. His figure, riding alongside her, was becoming a dark shadow as twilight fell.

"If you'd carried on that day when you found me, and left me for dead, it would have been better for you. No one would be in danger because of me," Josh said.

Amy was exhausted. Although she had adapted to life out West, no girl could readily recover from the sight of a charred body. She felt that this had all been discussed amongst the others in the general store after the explosion. There was no need for Josh to bring it up now, Much as she would have liked to snap back at Josh, she knew it wouldn't be fair; she ignored his remarks and changed the subject altogether.

"Do you think Ben and Pa would have found any

treasure today?" The question from Amy surprised Josh. But he realized she wanted to change the subject, and he was quite willing to do so.

"I shall be annoyed if they do. Perhaps even upset if they find gold bars and jewellery after just one day," said Josh.

"You'd be upset?" Amy was aghast. What a horrible thing to say, "Why? It would be wonderful for my father and Ben to find treasure so quickly."

"Just remember all those days and nights we have been out searching for the Jesuit treasure. Think of all those maps and instructions your father gave us. And all the false clues! Don't forget the flash flood we nearly drowned in, or the booby-trapped cave with the rocks that just missed hitting and killing us. I think it would be most unfair if they spent only one day searching and scooped a fantastic treasure after all our efforts brought us nothing."

Amy's laughter pealed out across the desert landscape. Josh joined in, realizing how little they had laughed recently. The last part of the journey was passed in a companionable silence. That nonsensical remark from Josh had lightened the mood between them and taken away the lingering horror of the day's events.

When they reached the ranch, it was with surprised greetings at their lateness from everyone there. The story—about the buggy, the explosion, and the renewed attacks upon Josh—was discussed again and again. Amy went out onto the porch, eager to get away from the talk. She was joined by Nancy, who had returned from a visit to Dry Creek Ranch.

"Had enough of the chat about it?" Nancy asked the girl.

"Yes, it was bad enough at the time, but this non-stop

talking about it makes it worse," said Amy, as settling herself on a chair on the porch.

Nancy withdrew from her pocket her cheroots. Shaking one out, she put the packet away and lit up. A deep breath, followed by slight coughing, and she puffed out the smoke. Settling back in one of the good chairs they had put on the porch, she gave a contented sigh. "That's better. I've been longing for this all day. My day has been difficult, Amy—not horrific, like yours, just difficult."

"Why? Is something wrong over at Dry Creek Ranch?" Amy twisted her chair around to look more closely at the older woman. Nancy had appeared some time ago and suggested a marriage of convenience between herself and Amy's father, Luke. Her husband had died some years before, leaving her the sole owner of Dry Creek Ranch. A corrupt sheriff and no-good bully had decided *he* wanted the ranch, and insisted she marry him. Nancy's marriage to Luke had thwarted that plan, but a gun battle afterwards had been needed to finalize the problem. For Nancy to find something difficult, Amy was perturbed. Never had the older woman confessed to any weakness at all.

"Well, Nancy, you can't just say that and not tell me all about it," insisted Amy. "Is it a problem with Sam and his family? I thought they were settling in well. After their escape from death from the bushwhacking man, they told me they were delighted to live on Dry Creek Ranch. What's happened? What's upset you?"

CHAPTER FORTY-ONE

Amy sat waiting patiently. She had only known Nancy for a short time, but she knew enough to realize that you had to wait for Nancy to continue speaking. Sometimes Nancy took her time thinking things out.

"It's that man. You met him, didn't you? The one who calls himself Jeremiah the Prophet. He has taken to calling at the Dry Creek Ranch. Hannah, Sam's mother, is a target for him to practise his vile language on her."

"Oh, yes. I've met him—he came into the general store. Told us all to kneel and repent of our sins. If we didn't, he said, he would call down God's wrath upon us. Nancy, you should have seen everybody's face. They were stunned. No one said anything at first. So, he began shouting at us all, and wandering up and down the store, yelling at us to get down on our knees," said Amy.

"What happened?" Nancy asked the girl. She hadn't heard this story about the prophet before and was utterly astonished at the sheer audacity of the man.

Amy began to chuckle and continued with the story, a huge grin on her face. "Manuel said he didn't need to repent; nor did Eliza, because they were both Catholic."

That made Jeremiah furious, and he shouted at them for being in thrall to the popish dogma and called the Pope a few rude names. Whereupon Manuel told him to get out. Eliza crossed herself in horror at these remarks about the Pope. Jeremiah left but, again, he promised the vengeance of the Lord upon them and their store.

"But Nancy, what do you mean? About Hannah being a target?" Amy was startled at this news from Nancy. They had met Sam, Hannah's son, an Apache half breed when he was riding with a group of Apache from his tribe. The Apache had been moved off their ancestral lands and were being forced into a reservation many miles away. The group had since split up, some travelling onto the reservation, others fleeing into the mountains away from Nowhere. Sam, his mother and younger brother had been persuaded to live on Dry Creek Ranch. David, the baby who dominated everyone's life since his arrival on Broken Horseshoe Ranch, was Hannah's grandson. Amy had discovered the baby when she and Josh were returning from a treasure hunt. David's parents, Hannah's daughter, along with her husband, had been murdered and left for dead.

"Why Hannah?" Amy asked again. "What has Hannah done to get such attention from him?"

Nancy began searching again in her pocket. Normally, each night she would only have one cheroot. But frustration and anger over the explosion to the buggy at the general store, and this new arrival of a so-called prophet attacking Hannah, was just too much for her. She needed another cheroot. She found the packet, took one out, and lit it—leaving Amy waiting impatiently for the answer to her question.

After a deep, indrawn breath, Nancy began speaking again: "It's because she's been living with the Apache. She was captured when she was fourteen. He said Hannah is a sinner; she has to repent and repudiate her sons and grandson. They should be banned from the ranch, as they originally come from an evil heathen sect." Nancy took another puff from the cheroot and blew out the smoke in an angry spiral. She leaned forward to tap the growing ash on the tip onto the ground beneath the porch.

Amy shivered. It was cooler now but, after the heat of

the day and the events that had occurred at the general store, she was still on edge. "Hannah is such a shy person. She carried a small Bible with her throughout her captivity and her life in the Indian village. I've never met such a true Christian. Hannah kept up her prayers and her faith through all the adversity she has suffered," said Amy.

"That's not all, Amy. That Jeremiah has warned her: if she doesn't drive Sam and Matthew away from the ranch or move in with him—Jeremiah—and his wife, evil will befall Dry Creek Ranch. When I arrived there, the man was shouting at her. Sam and Matthew were out seeing to the animals, and Nat was the only person there to help her. Jeremiah shouted at Nat as well."

Nancy suddenly stood up and threw away the stub of the cheroot after stamping it out underfoot. She began pacing up and down the porch. Her anxiety at this man's behaviour was intense. "Would you believe it, Amy? He shouted at Nat and said his evil ways must have cost him his leg. Losing his leg during the Civil War was obviously Nat's fault, and he must have deserved it." Nancy came to a sudden stop in front of Amy. "I wanted to shoot that man dead on the spot, or at least in his leg! I could see Nat's hand reaching for his gun. Just as I reached for mine. Luckily for that man, both Nat and I smiled at each other, realizing what we both wanted to do. We started laughing. That took Jeremiah aback. Eventually, he left. But Hannah was nearly hysterical, weeping bitterly. She didn't want to believe him, but that Jeremiah is a powerful speaker and uses many Bible quotes to back up his evil speechifying."

Amy sat silent for a moment, staring intently at Nancy. The words seemed to rattle about in her brain. She had met the man, had disliked him, and even felt threatened by him and his powerful ranting. There was no arguing with the man; there was no way of shouting him down. Sheriff Grey was powerless against him: he was breaking no laws.

"What can we do to help her? There must be *something* that we can do? There is no way I'm leaving her at that man's mercy!" Amy declared.

CHAPTER FORTY-TWO

Unknown to Nancy and Amy, their raised voices had been heard by the others, who had gathered at the open door and stood listening. "Bring her here, to Broken Horseshoe Ranch. We can keep her safe here," said Luke, walking out onto the porch.

"She won't come, Luke. I offered to bring her back here myself. She knows Dry Creek Ranch from when they camped beneath the mesa, and beside the small stream. Hannah finds it familiar and cannot cope with anywhere else strange. I hate to say this, but Hannah is almost at a breaking point. Dry Creek Ranch is her one chance of her family settling down, with Sam, running the place and Matthew helping him. She is determined that they find a new way of living and feels she can't do anything to jeopardize that."

"But that's ridiculous!" Luke said. "We're not asking her to come here permanently," he said.

Nancy nodded her head. "I know that, but she won't agree, Luke. What also worries me is that Sam is the only fit man able to withstand an attack. If this figure Nat has seen skulking around at night tries anything, Sam might struggle on his own. Matthew is too young and Nat, of course, isn't fully able to take part in a fight," Nancy said.

"Tomorrow, Amy and I won't be working at the general store. We'll go over there and stay for a couple of days. That might help," said Josh.

Both Ezra and Bill had come around to the cabin at the sound of the raised voices, Leah, Ezra's wife, hurrying up behind them. Bill had previously worked for Nancy at Dry Creek Ranch. Losing an arm in the Civil War, he now wielded a hook but was limited in his physical work.

When Luke discovered he had been a professor in an eastern university, he was brought over to Broken Horseshoe Ranch to tutor Ben. With the child no longer at school, Luke worried about his youngest falling behind in academic work. Ben did not worry about that at all!

"How about I go back to Dry Creek Ranch? There's very little more I can teach Ben. He's reached a high standard and can carry on his own. I can be of more use if I return to Dry Creek." Bill looked hopefully at Nancy. Truth to tell, he preferred Dry Creek Ranch. When he was there, he shared a broken-down hut made of sod and discarded bleached wood found in the desert with Nat. Leah and Ezra had made him welcome in their small cabin, but he missed the camaraderie of Nat and the happy hours spent together with a bottle of whiskey! Leah and Ezra had lived for many years at Broken Horseshoe Ranch, and had welcomed the new owners, Luke, and his family. Luke's family survived their early months at Broken Horseshoe Ranch, thanks to Leah and Ezra's knowledge and experience of the foothills of Devil's Mountain.

"Yes, that would be a temporary solution," said Luke. "We'll see what happens in the next few days. But that Jeremiah must be sorted out. No way can he visit Hannah and her family if he is going to shout and abuse them."

That was settled—especially to Nancy's satisfaction. Dry Creek Ranch had been her property, and she still felt it was up to her to ensure the smooth running of it. They all drifted off to bed, Bill happily packing a bag ready for his return to Dry Creek Ranch. Amy, going to sleep in her cupboard bedroom, crept slowly—and as quietly as possible— to her bed. David was asleep (lying with his chubby arms still for once) in the large wooden drawer from Nancy's bureau.

"David, wait until you wake up in the morning. I've got a surprise for you," whispered Amy.

CHAPTER FORTY-THREE

Amy remembered those whispered words to David as she went to bed. In the cold light of morning, she regretted every one of them. The baby hadn't heard them and, if he had, he wouldn't have understood what she meant by it. So, she hadn't really promised it. She could always change her mind.

"I thought we should take David with us. Surely seeing him will help Hannah?"

"That's a good idea," Nancy enthused. "She hasn't seen him for ages. He's her grandson and he should really get to know her."

Everyone agreed that taking David with her to Dry Creek Ranch would be just the thing to brighten Hannah's day. Except, it wasn't brightening Amy's day. Not one little bit. The baby somehow understood that today was going to be different. So, he decided it was the perfect day to be difficult and awkward. Getting him washed and dressed took Amy, Leah and Nancy all together an unbelievable time, trying to get his clothes on ready for the journey. They were hurrying, anxious to get the baby settled at Dry Creek Ranch before the intense heat of the day built up.

Having the buggy destroyed in the explosion at the general store meant that everything David needed, indeed David himself, had to be carried on horseback.

"I've harnessed Star, and Bella is ready for you," Ben said, leading both horses round to the porch hitching rail.

"One of the old nags that those bandits left behind will do for me," said Bill. He joined the other horses, his belongings in two saddlebags and already on his horse. "I can strap on some more bundles for you to take with us to

Dry Creek," he added.

Leah had brought an old cotton blanket into the cabin. "David needs to be wrapped up firmly in this so that he is easier for you to carry. Once we get him in it, we can fashion a sling and loop it over the top of your head. That way, he will be secure and close to you. Once you get going, I'm sure he will fall asleep with the movement."

Amy looked down at the wriggling baby. His cherubic face held a hint of mischief, even for such a young baby. The cotton gown he wore was being kicked up in all directions. The bonnet that Leah had carefully made, and placed on his head earlier, had been torn off in one tiny hand, and was being waved about furiously.

"I'm not carrying that baby on a horse." Josh stood in the doorway, leaning against the doorjamb with a huge grin on his face. He flicked his hair back, and his eyes sparkled with an unholy joy at the look of horror on Amy's face, as she wondered how she was going to cope with the active David on horseback.

Bill had come up behind Josh and was looking through the door at the womenfolk in the cabin tending the baby. He poked Josh in the ribs with his hook. "Reckon this is a first time that I've been glad not to have had two arms. I might have had to hold the baby otherwise." He roared with laughter at his remark and, to Amy's fury, Josh joined in.

With the saddlebags full and bundles tied onto Josh and Bill's horses, they helped Amy onto her horse with David. The sling was over her head and tied round her back, and David was snuggled into it. His eyes were wide open at the unexpected novelty of sitting in Amy's lap on a horse.

"He was quieter the last time you carried him on

horseback," murmured Josh. He glanced down at the child and stroked his cheek, and looked at Amy. For a moment, their gazes held as they remembered. It all came back to Amy: the broken bodies of David's parents sprawled in the dirt, murdered by bandits. His mother, fleeing from the murderers, had hidden David. It had taken Leah and Amy many sleepless nights to keep the newborn child alive.

"Yes, he was much quieter on that day," Amy murmured. That was all they said. But the depth of the experience they had gone through lingered in the solemn faces they both wore as they gazed down at David.

Josh, now mounted, looked at Bill and Amy. "Ready. Let's get to Dry Creek Ranch. Hannah shouldn't be left on her on her own with Nat any longer."

"If that man Jeremiah comes back, he'll get a shock to find us there, ready and waiting for him," Amy said.

Leah had been quite correct. David soon fell asleep with the constant repetitive motion of the horse. Smiling down at him, Amy saw the faint beads of perspiration on his dewy cheeks and upper lip. His blond curls were damp as he sweated in the increasing heat.

"Not long now—we'll see Dry Creek Ranch over the next ridge," said Josh. He was trying to encourage Amy, whom he could tell was finding the constant burden of the baby difficult and tiring whilst riding the horse.

It was Bill who reached the top of the ridge first. He halted and turned back to the other two, and shouted at them: "Hurry! We must hurry. I see smoke rising on the horizon! There's a fire at Dry Creek Ranch!"

CHAPTER FORTY-FOUR

That initial surprise of the plume of smoke in the distance made them rein in their horses and pause for a moment as they tried to work out what they were actually seeing on the horizon.

"Stay back with David," Josh called to Amy, and he and Bill rode as fast as they could towards Dry Creek Ranch and the smoke drifting up in the sky.

Amy trotted after them, wishing that she could join with them in a mad dash, but appreciated Josh's advice on staying back with David. It would be stupid to run into trouble with a small baby. Her anxious eyes watched the two figures as they grew further away from her.

Her steady pace eventually brought her and David up to the ranch itself, her anxious eyes seeking for a sight of Hannah and Nat. It was with relief she saw them both gesticulating wildly beside the two horsemen that had joined them.

"They're both safe and unharmed, Amy." Josh's voice carried towards her, reinforcing Amy's relief. The ranch could be built again, but she had seen too many people wounded and dead lately. Death, and wounds inflicted on people, too often couldn't be remedied. The thought of Hannah, and the gentle character of Nat, being hurt had frightened her.

Smoke was drifting slowly skywards, gradually lessening in volume as Amy looked towards its source. The small hut that had belonged to the two Civil War veterans and had been built painstakingly by them with an assortment of wood and sod, had been set alight. That was what was still burning and had sent the smoke plume into the sky. The last embers of the small cabin were drifting upwards and giving the smoke a dirty grey colour.

"Is there any damage to the ranch itself?" Amy queried as she reached the group standing on the porch in front of the ranch.

"We're fine, Amy. I can't understand it, because we heard nothing. When we woke this morning, it was to find the small cabin up in flames. Nat had slept in the ranch house itself last night. It seemed safer for both of us to be together after he had seen someone skulking around at dusk. Thank goodness he was with me. I hate to think what would have happened to him if he had been sleeping out there," Hannah said, pointing to the debris left by the blaze, as she began walking towards the girl as Amy rode up to the porch.

Hannah's eyes widened. She put a hand up to her mouth as she looked more closely at Amy, who was still on the horse. Her eyes were fixed on the large bundle Amy held tightly as she rode up on Bella. Hannah stepped forward, her hand on the rail to steady herself as she looked at the sleeping child held in Amy's arms. "Is it? Is that David?" she whispered, tiptoeing the last few steps towards Amy.

"No, it's some other baby I found on the way here," teased Amy. "Can you help me? If you can reach out and take him, I can slide him out of my sling."

The older woman reached out her arms willingly, a delighted smile on her face as she looked down at the sleeping child. David murmured as he was passed from one person to the other, but he didn't wake. His grandmother held him tight in her arms, one hand reaching up to smooth the blonde curls away from his face. Hannah turned and looked at Amy. The radiant smile upon the older woman's face was enough thanks for Amy. It made her aching arms and stiff back worthwhile.

"Thank you for bringing him," Hannah whispered before she took him inside to the cool darkness of the cabin.

Amy jumped down from Bella, patting the horse and whispering her gratitude towards her as usual. Then, she walked across to stand beside the men looking at the smouldering ruins. Her heart ached for Bill and Nat as both men—wounded badly in the last days of the terrible war that had been waged across America—stood looking at their former home.

"I'm sorry, I know it was only small, but you both built up a home that you both loved and were comfortable in," she whispered.

"That's bad enough, Miss Amy, but have you seen what's writ on the side of the ranch house?" Nat pointed, his face becoming a mask of anger.

"The fire was deliberate and carries a message from the person who set it." Bill stood beside his soldier friend, an angry frown creasing his face.

"Repent! That's painted on the wall. Isn't that what Jeremiah shouted at you and Hannah?" Amy whirled round towards Nat. "It must have been him. The prophet must have painted it and started the fire."

"He'll deny it. Didn't you hear about one of those new homesteaders, Miss Amy? The homesteader wouldn't pray with him, and told Jeremiah to clear off, and eventually threatened him with a gun. His wagon burned down the next day, and the word repent was painted on his cabin. Sheriff Grey went out but couldn't prove anything," Bill said, shaking his head at the petty vindictiveness of the prophet.

"What does Jeremiah say?" Amy asked.

"I reckon you're going to find out exactly what Jeremiah says," Josh said, and pointed at the dust cloud coming towards them—with Jeremiah, his wife and son seated in the buggy and fast approaching Dry Creek Ranch.

Nat said, "Now, we'll see what Jeremiah has to say for himself."

CHAPTER FORTY-FIVE

The wagon drew up in front of the porch and the group that had congregated there. Hannah, with baby David in her arms, stood in the doorway of the ranch house. Not one of the assembled group spoke; they were waiting to see what the so-called prophet, Jeremiah, was going to do and say.

His wife sat hunched beside him. The huge bonnet not only shielded her face from the sun, but it also concealed it entirely from view. A plain drab dress was worn beneath a shawl, which (to Amy) looked as if it had been crocheted with straw.

The tall, white-bearded man, with long, flowing white hair, climbed down from the buggy and walked towards them.

"God has spoken! I see vengeance and retribution have come upon you sinners." His loud booming voice echoed across the empty arid land. Reaching the smouldering remnants of the hut, he stood for a moment looking at it and then gave a joyful shout, throwing his arms up towards the sky. "I warned them! Oh Lord, I warned them to repent of their sins, to leave their wicked ways, and cast out the heathens from their dwelling place!"

Amy gave a loud snort of laughter at this remark.

The man whirled round in an instant and stepped towards her. His eyes flashed with an almost maniacal fire in them as they swept up and down the girl's figure. He lifted his cane and shook it at her. "You harlot! You are nothing but a strumpet! Why are you not wearing a bonnet and covering your hair modestly? Your skirt is too short and its length shows that you are a fallen woman, fit only to be strutting on the streets!"

These remarks were met by a stunned silence. They were unexpected, cruel, and extreme in so many different ways.

Jeremiah took another step closer to Amy. He lifted his cane and brought it down, getting it ready to strike her across the head. First, he looked up to the sky, shouting the following words: "I shall chastise the woman! I shall bring her before the Lord as a penitent sinner, and she shall repent her sins. Repent, Jezebel!" These words were yelled in his usual loud voice but ended in a thundering roar as the cane began to descend upon Amy.

The cane did not descend upon Amy's head. It was wrenched away from Jeremiah. It caught him unawares and threw him off-balance. He staggered to one side before regaining his balance.

Bill had moved silently and unexpectedly fast. "No one hits a woman. No man, be he Christian or heathen, would ever hit a young woman as you were about to. I didn't lose my arm in a war to find bullies like you at large, preying on defenceless women!" Bill stood there. The cane had been wrenched from Jeremiah's grasp by his metal hook and had landed some distance away. The normally quiet man stood there, his hook raised threateningly at Jeremiah.

Josh, who had been momentarily shocked, and had not expected the physical assault upon Amy, moved forward to stand in front of her. He wasn't worried about Jeremiah attacking her again. Oh no! One look at Amy's face, and the hand that had reached in the pocket of her skirt for her knife, made him fearful. Not for her safety, for he knew how proficient Amy was with a knife. No—Josh was worried she might show just how proficient she was with it on Jeremiah.

The large, imposing figure of Jeremiah loomed over Nat and Bill, along with his sullen son, a beefy young man. These veterans and Hannah would not have stood a chance physically against them, Josh realized.

After the explosion and demolition of their buggy at the general store, Josh had fully intended to leave Nowhere, and the Broken Horseshoe Ranch. He felt he was bringing danger and death to everyone by his very presence. Josh still thought that he brought some element of danger into their lives. But, as he looked at the two men—Jeremiah and his son, and their powerful physical presence—he realized he was needed. Josh was the only fully bodied and able man amongst them: Nat and Bill were handicapped by their injuries sustained in the Civil War. They would be capable of so much in the defence of Hannah and Amy, but it would be an uneven fight. Now, more than ever, Josh felt that his presence (along with Amy's) evened up any fight that might erupt.

"Damn you! How dare you strike a man of God in pursuit of the will of the Bible!" Jeremiah spat these words out at Bill. He bent over and picked up his cane, shaking it in the air at each one of them. "Vengeance is mine, saith the Lord. I promise you: vengeance will come upon each one of you." At that, he stalked off towards his buggy.

It was Amy who looked towards the woman, whereas all other eyes were fixed on Jeremiah himself. Amy saw the woman's head lift, and how she looked straight at her husband. Hatred sparked from the woman's eyes towards the man and a grim expression flitted across her worn, tired face. Amy shuddered at the venomous look Jeremiah received. She had seen first-hand how the man could turn to violence. Bill's hook had wrenched the cane from the man's hand as he was about to hit her with it. She had been prepared to duck away from him. Her hand had already been reaching for her knife before Bill acted. But she had to admit: the man had taken her unawares, and he possibly would have succeeded in delivering a blow.

The buggy was driven away from Dry Creek Ranch by the son. A sly, simpering look crossed his face as he looked at each one of them, and the ranch house itself, before driving off towards the plot of land they had newly bought and were attempting to settle on.

"Thank you, Bill! You got the cane from him. Well done! And you told him off." Amy flung her arms around the old soldier, giving him a big hug. "Thank goodness he's gone."

"But I don't think we've heard the last of him. Do you, Josh?" Bill asked as they all turned to walk back to the ranch house.

Josh replied thoughtfully. "No, the man needs watching. I think we need to be on alert. He hasn't finished with Dry Creek Ranch. He'll be back, perhaps another sneak attack at night. I don't think that we have seen the last of Jeremiah, the so-called prophet."

CHAPTER FORTY-SIX

That night was spent by the men taking the guard duty, one after the other. Amy was too involved with Hannah and David to be included in the patrols around the ranch house. The strange surroundings and the unusual voices had made the baby cranky. They were all relieved when he finally dozed off that evening.

"Thank you for bringing him over to see me," Hannah said as both women sat in front of the stove that night. The evening air was cooler, and the warmth of the stove was welcome. It was also kept alight to keep the coffee pot refreshed throughout the night, so necessary to keep the men awake and warm them up.

Nat was still doing the cooking. He enjoyed it and, despite the upset of the day and his distress at the loss of his home, he produced a tasty stew. He and Hannah, since her arrival at Dry Creek Ranch, had worked hard on Nancy's garden, and despite the loss of keen gardener Rosita and her two sons it flourished. The big bedroom that the Mexican family had slept in, was used that night by Amy, Hannah, and David. The small room was given over to Ezra and Josh, who were taking it in turns to patrol the ranch. Nat and Bill were quite happy sleeping on the porch after their turn at guard duty.

"The things that man said to you were so false and cruel," said Hannah to Amy. "He must have upset you." The delicate embroidery that Hannah was doing on a piece of linen was put to one side. She stared at the young girl sitting beside her. "Do you want to talk about it?" The soft, gentle voice of Hannah revealed how worried she was that Jeremiah's remarks might have hurt the young girl.

Amy, taken unawares by these remarks, took a moment to answer Hannah. "Goodness, Hannah, that silly old fool's remarks didn't upset me at all. But I *am* angry that Bill got his cane out of his hand before I did. My hand was reaching for the knife in my pocket." Her brows knit together, the freckles making an almost unbroken path across her nose as she screwed up her face with fury at the thought of Jeremiah.

"You didn't let his remarks the other day upset *you*, did you, Hannah?" Amy asked the older woman in turn.

"I was ..." Hannah did not finish her reply. She didn't need to. The telltale blush rising from her neck and up her cheeks, flooding her face, made it obvious to Amy that Jeremiah's remarks had destroyed the fragile woman's peace.

Amy jumped to her feet and began pacing up and down the small room in her frustration. "That man is poison! Sheriff Grey will have to run him out of town. How *dare* he treat me like he did, and accuse you of evil? As if you had any choice in the matter! You didn't ask to be captured by the Apache, did you?" The pacing stopped abruptly and Amy stood over the startled Hannah.

"As if anything that happened to you was by your own doing. It wasn't, was it? You couldn't help any of it at all. And how could he expect you to send your sons away and ignore them?" demanded Amy.

"No, no, I didn't, I couldn't ..." Hannah's face puckered and tears filled her eyes.

Amy, who had resumed her pacing, stopped in mid stride and looked down at Hannah. Seated in the chair, Hannah wiped her eyes and sniffed. Realisation swept over the girl. This woman was fragile. Amy, for all her innocence and youth, was much the stronger of the two of them.

Kneeling down beside her chair, Amy put her arms around the woman. "I'm so sorry, Hannah. I didn't mean to upset you. Please forgive me." Hugging the woman, Amy discovered that not only was Hannah fragile emotionally but she was also thin and undernourished. At that moment, Amy decided Hannah would not only survive to enjoy life at Dry Creek Ranch but she would also flourish and thrive.

Hannah whispered into Amy's ear. "I'm crying because you are so kind. Amy, you are the first white woman to really understand what happened to me. That man and his prejudices towards me are what I expected to encounter from all the so-called normal people in Nowhere. We hoped to live here without my coming into contact with anyone." The words flooding out of the distraught woman touched Amy's heart.

"You needn't meet up with anyone in the town, Hannah. We can make sure that you stay here and enjoy your life without bothering with anyone else. But, if you feel you want to meet people, I can always come with you. No, the first time you go into town, Nancy and I will be by your side. I doubt anybody will say a cross word to you or insult you—not with both of us beside you!" Amy sat back on her heels, the look of determination on her face at odds with her snub nose and freckles. "They wouldn't dare!"

CHAPTER FORTY-SEVEN

Next morning, Nat got an early breakfast ready for them all, happy to work with the pots and pans in the tiny kitchen area. Despite their night duty, the men were quite cheerful and refreshed. Not so Amy and Hannah. Well aware of the unsettling events of the day and the anxiety of the surrounding adults, David had been difficult throughout the night.

"Manuel is expecting me this morning to help with the deliveries. I should really go in and help him, Amy," Josh said as he downed his second cup of coffee.

"I've accounts to do, but Dora is there to help Eliza in the general store. The business in the hardware section counts for very little at the moment. I could do the accounts anywhere. If they could be brought back here, I could work on them during the day and even at nighttime. That way, I could help Hannah in the garden, and with David, and be an extra gun to protect Dry Creek Ranch until Sam gets back," Amy said as she tried to spoon some breakfast into David's mouth. She backed away as he prepared to spit it out at her.

"Here Amy, let me take him, whilst you have your breakfast." Nat had eaten his breakfast whilst cooking everyone else's, and he sat down beside her and held out his arms for the baby.

David stared at the unfamiliar face in front of him. It puzzled him, especially Nat's whiskers, of which Nat was extremely proud. Since coming to the ranch, he had cultivated two large, curling whiskers that joined the sideboards growing down the sides of his face.

A chubby hand reached out to touch the luxuriant hair regrowth. Everyone laughed at this. David looked round in surprise. Nat took the opportunity to lift him off Amy and onto his own good knee, skilfully dropping a spoonful of breakfast into the baby's mouth.

"We need more provisions here. I should take the buggy in with you, Josh, and stock up. We have more mouths to feed now and my shelves are getting bare," said Nat, spooning the last of the breakfast into the baby's mouth.

"I can shoot a rifle and a gun," said Hannah. "I don't like to, but if it means defending Dry Creek Ranch, and ourselves, I'm quite willing to have a go."

"What if Nat and Josh go into Nowhere in the buggy, and Nat stocks up with supplies for the ranch—and also the account work I have to do—and then he comes straight back? You, Josh, can borrow a nag from the livery stables and ride back here at the end of the day. Would that work?" Amy said as she collected the dirty breakfast bowls for washing.

"I can be back in no time at all, if we leave at once," said Nat, handing David to Hannah.

Josh drained his coffee to the very last dregs and frowned: "But it only leaves Bill, Amy, and Hannah to defend themselves on the ranch. I don't like it. I don't trust that Jeremiah not to come back and cause trouble."

"If you two get going, we can get all the outside chores done right away and then settle into the cabin and on the front porch. That way, we can barricade ourselves in if need be. We will have the guns and rifles ready for action," Amy said.

With that, Josh had to be content, and he and Nat were soon driving down the trail from Dry Creek Ranch into Nowhere. He glanced back and was pleased to see that Amy, Hannah, and Bill were scurrying around, seeing to the animals and working in the garden. The boxes in the back of the buggy held fresh vegetables and fruit from Nancy's garden. Amy was right, Josh thought, they had to go to Nowhere that very day otherwise Nancy's produce would not survive. And Nancy was someone you didn't want to get upset or cross about her produce going to waste.

The journey passed quickly. Between the two men, the conversation was easy and about nothing much in general. They stabled the horse and left the buggy outside the stable, ready to load. Josh carried most of the boxes into the general store, with Nat coming up behind him with the last of them.

"Good. I'm so pleased you got here. Our supplies of fresh fruit and vegetable have run low. Eliza will be delighted to put these in the baskets on the boardwalk. Where's Amy? Not with you, Josh? She's not ill, I hope?" Manuel took one box from Josh and carried it further into the store, placing it on a table for Eliza to look over. Every box was counted and entered up in a book to credit Nancy and the Dry Creek Ranch.

"We had some bother at Dry Creek Ranch with that so-called prophet, Jeremiah," Josh said.

Manuel shook his head, and Eliza spoke up: "Not you as well. He has upset so many people. The latest man to be upset is Seth at the saloon. Jeremiah stood outside, turning his customers away, and telling Seth he was the devil's spawn for selling alcohol."

"I'll bet that didn't go down well!" laughed Josh. He could imagine the irate Seth discovering his customers were being turned away. "I'll bet Seth had something to say to him."

"Yes, but Jeremiah had an answer. He said that God

171

would strike Seth and his saloon down, and Seth had to prepare for the destruction of the Lord."

Josh's face hardened. He dug his hands into the pockets of his jacket, hiding his clenched fists from the others. He wouldn't easily forget the sight of Jeremiah's cane over Amy's head in a hurry. Then, he and Nat told of the drama that had unfolded at Dry Creek Ranch, and the fire that had destroyed Bill and Nat's small cabin.

"So you see, Manuel, Amy is staying there to help Hannah with the baby, and to help protect them and the ranch from further attacks. She asked if Nat could take the accounts to the ranch with him, and would you be willing for her to work on them back there?" Josh said.

"No problem at all. Amy can sort them out. There're two piles here: the general stores accounts and now the ones from the saloon. They can go in these canvas sacks for her. Best take a supply of pen, nibs, and ink as well."

Nat gathered together all the provisions necessary for the increased company at Dry Creek Ranch. Josh helped him carry them down the buggy, along with the accounts for Amy. They walked back up into the general store for Nat to pick up the last box.

"What is it? What do you think you're doing? Don't you shove me!" The first shouts came from a single voice, then voices were raised in protest. Then there could be heard the sound of blows, and the fighting began. Manuel and Josh rushed out of the general store to find a group of miners fighting on the boardwalk in front of the store.

"Never mind the fighting, Nat—you get back to Dry Creek Ranch!" Josh shouted at the man as he made to follow them out of the door. He gave Nat a push back into the store, closing the door on him. As Josh turned back, a punch from a meaty fist sent him flying off the boardwalk and into the dusty street.

CHAPTER FORTY-EIGHT

Josh lay in the dirt and rubbed his jaw where the punch had connected. "That hurt," he groaned.

A look around showed him a group of men fighting one another. To his dismay, he saw the hardware objects and vegetables that Eliza and Dora had arranged with such care on the boardwalk, being used as missiles and weapons.

The men were fighting each other, but they were also grabbing anything at hand to inflict pain upon their opponents. They were mostly the miners from the silver mines up in the mountains. But there were a few—mainly grizzled old-timers—who searched and panned for gold in the canyons around the Devil's Mountains. Each and every man of them had joined in enthusiastically, swinging wildly at their opponents.

The silver miners were a rough-looking crew. Most of their faces were obscured by wild, unruly beards, and their skin, where it could be seen, was dirt-stained. They were clad in tattered clothing, torn and worn through by their constant hard labour. The owners of some of the silver mines were grasping and greedy, forcing their men to work long hours. Coming into town was a way of letting off steam after their hard work. Some miners lived isolated lives, only coming into contact with people on the rare occasions they actually ventured into town. Duloe was their usual town of choice but, despite the lack of stores and saloons, its shorter journey made Nowhere an easier option.

Groggily, Josh rose to his feet and made his way past the fighting men up to the boardwalk itself. Two men were grappling with each other, neither giving way, blundering into the scattered boxes they had knocked to the ground.

"Go and fight in the street!" he shouted at them, but they ignored him, still wrestling with each other. Josh grabbed one of the metal pans used for sifting out the precious ore found in many of the streams and canyons high in the mountains. Lifting it up above his head, Josh brought it down on the shoulders of one man, and then, as the miner twisted and grunted at this blow from behind him, Josh hit him again sideways, this time knocking him into the street. Still holding his grappling partner, both unwilling to let go, the fighting men hurtled onto the street. For a moment, Josh watched them, shaking his head as their sudden descent into the dirt and dust didn't stop their need to continue to fight each other.

Still holding his now trusty, unorthodox weapon, Josh launched forward with it raised up high above his head. He had caught sight of a scruffy miner slipping up onto the boardwalk and saw that the man was about to make off with a couple of shovels.

"Oh, no, you don't! You leave that stuff where it belongs. Clear off, you thief!" Josh shouted, and again hit out with his metal pan. He clipped the man on the shoulder, who gave a yell of pain. Dropping the shovels, he jumped from the boardwalk and ran off. Josh stood triumphantly, waving his metal pan in the air as he was now the sole survivor on the boardwalk.

Again, Sheriff Lance Grey strode into the midst of the men. He raised both guns and fired them above the fighting men's heads. "I'm not having this in my town! Fight on your claims. Knock each other senseless out at the silver mine. Those of you searching for gold: stay out of my town if you're set on coming into Nowhere looking for trouble. Next time I'll shoot legs and arms, not up in the air!"

The men had, by now, drawn apart from their opponents and were sorting out the injuries they were discovering on their bodies. They began drifting away from each other. Someone, making certain that Sheriff Grey didn't see who it was, shouted out at him: "What about those bars on the window, Sheriff? Still got an open window in your jail?"

A ripple of laughter swept through the crowd, gaining strength as it was repeated amongst the Nowhere onlookers. A crowd of the local townspeople had gathered to see the fight. They, too, laughed at these remarks. The continuing argument between the blacksmith and the sheriff had stopped the making of the sheriff's metal cell window bars.

Sheriff Grey drew himself up and cast a steely glare around the onlookers and the fighting men. The entire crowd fell silent. The man's powerful personality ensured that he gained everyone's attention.

"Don't need a jail cell with bars on the window. No need for bars. Got a new man moved into town. He's an undertaker. We got plenty of room up on the hill to bury folks." This was said with a smile, and Sheriff Grey gave a laugh. In fact, he found it so funny he doubled over with laughter, slapping his thighs with merriment.

Not one other person joined in with his laughter. Josh, watching from the doorway of the general store, felt his blood run cold at the chilling sound of it.

CHAPTER FORTY-NINE

Manuel opened the door of the general store behind Josh. Manuel wore a sheepish expression on his face but was held back by Eliza's hand gripping his arm. "She wouldn't let me come out and fight," Manuel apologized to Josh.

"I saw no reason for him to be involved with a stupid fight amongst those miners!" Eliza said, and glared at Josh, daring him to object.

Josh hid his smile at the chagrined expression on Manuel's face. "Quite right, Eliza—there was no need for Manuel to join in. I had no option. I walked out of the store and got punched right out onto the dirt of Main Street. That got me mad and, before I knew it, I was in the middle of it," said Josh.

Dora had joined the group now, standing on the porch. She grinned at Josh. "That was pretty fancy work with the pan." She indicated the metal pan Josh was still holding. "You going to go gold prospecting next?"

Realizing that he still had a tight hold on the metal pan, Josh, embarrassed at his former actions of waving it in the air triumphantly, placed it on the table. which normally held the vegetables and fruit. "I got mad when I saw them making a mess of all this stuff." He gestured towards the damaged fruit and vegetables that were not only across the boardwalk but scattered about Main Street itself.

Manuel looked about him at the mess and damage caused by the miners and their fighting, and shrugged his shoulders. "I've lost money with these damaged goods, but I can't complain. These miners bring in a lot of money for the store when they buy provisions and mining equipment from me. I reckon, if I want their money I have to put up with their nonsense." He gave another shrug of his shoulders and began picking up the metal hardware implements that were lying scattered everywhere. "But I think it's best we keep everything safe in the store from now on."

All the onlookers—the battered and bruised miners and the last few gold prospectors—had drifted away. Sheriff Grey stood in the middle of Main Street with a satisfied look on his face. As he prepared to go back to his office, he saw the group standing outside the general store. "Any fresh coffee going, Eliza?" he called up to her.

"Certainly, Sheriff! I'll brew up a fresh pot for you." Eliza scurried back into the store and could be heard clattering about, getting freshly brewed coffee for the sheriff.

"You're not keeping these goods outside again, are you, Manuel?" Sheriff Grey asked as he joined them. "They made a real mess out here, didn't they?"

"I was just saying, Sheriff, it's the last time they'll get put out here. Everything will be safely behind the doors from now on," Manuel said. He and Josh continued picking up the rest of the stuff from the street and boardwalk. .

Leaning back in his chair, Sheriff Grey swallowed the scalding hot coffee with delight. Josh drank his coffee, but only after he'd blown on it to take the scalding heat off it. He found the man sitting opposite him, wearing his badge of office, a puzzle. On first coming into Nowhere, the man had been the preacher. Each Sunday he had given a sermon and prayed over the congregation with powerful oratory. The man had known his Bible and quoted it in a voice of authority, although Sunday worship was always held in the saloon. And he always had a glass of whiskey to help the words of the Bible along.

When the former corrupt sheriff had disappeared, presumed dead in the mountains, no one else would take his place. The few people living in Nowhere at that time decided that the preacher would make a decent sheriff, so now he was their permanent sheriff. The man had authority and the charismatic presence needed to carry off the sheriff's position with ease. He was also handy with his guns. Again and again, Josh wondered about this man. Where had he come from? What was in his past? Never did Sheriff Lance Grey mention anything, or anyone, from his past life.

The sheriff began speaking. He held his cup in his hands, twisting it round and round as he spoke.

"Called out early this morning by one of those new homesteaders. He'd had an argument with that man, Jeremiah, the day before. Jeremiah had arrived at his place, threatened him, telling him that the Lord would strike him down if he didn't get on his knees and pray with him." Taking another sip of his coffee, the sheriff glanced at his cup, realizing it was empty. A sorrowful look crept over his face.

That was all Eliza needed. She jumped to her feet. "A second cup?" Eliza asked, and began pouring it.

The cup was held out to her, and Sheriff Grey nodded his thanks and continued with his story. "That night, the man was looking for a lost goat. Doesn't know what he's doing with animals, but knew he had to get it back before a predator got it. On his search, he got lost in one of the small canyons on the edge of his property. Sensibly, he threw down his bedroll and slept where he was. Woke up to find the wretched goat asleep beside him."

Manuel and Dora had been checking over the fruit and vegetables they had retrieved from the boardwalk and the street, whilst listening to the story. Those goods too damaged to sell had been placed in one basket. The others were being wiped over by Eliza and Josh, getting them clean of the dust and dirt. Luckily, given that they had been used as missiles and weapons, few were too damaged for selling.

Eliza became impatient at this long-winded story from Sheriff Grey. She wanted to know what he'd been called out for. "What happened? What was the wrath of God that attacked his homestead?"

CHAPTER FIFTY

The long legs of the sheriff stretched out across the wooden floor. Josh noticed the boots he always wore, highly polished black ones, with silver inlaid motifs up the sides of them. Every morning, the man was immaculately dressed in his black outfit. Josh also noticed the guns. No matter how the man stood or sat, they were always ready for him to draw at a moment's notice.

"The same fire and warning sign was painted on a wall, just as happened at Dry Creek Ranch. An outbuilding was burned down and 'Repent' painted on a remaining wall. Seems these prophecies of Jeremiah all follow the same destructive pattern."

Eliza paused in her task and exclaimed. "That poor man, he's only just moved in here. He knows nothing about how to cope with the land and his animals. This is terrible. How will he manage after this setback?"

"Did he catch the goat? Is it safe?" Dora asked the question that she thought was most important. She ignored the smirk that crossed Sheriff Grey's face.

"Yes, the goat is safe. It stayed with him when he woke. But I have to agree with you, Eliza. It's a massive blow to this man. Not the sort of start to your new life that you'd wish for." The sheriff rose to his feet, handed the cup to Eliza with a nod of thanks, and stalked out of the general store.

"Best get our deliveries done, now that the excitement is over. I don't think you'll have any further bother with the miners today, Eliza. Most of them have gone back to work," Manuel said as he placed the last shovels, picks and panning supplies in the wooden bins he used for storing them. The heavier items he hung on hooks or had placed up against the wall. It had been a leap of faith for him to invest in these items and expand the general store with a hardware area. But the new influx of prospectors and miners into Nowhere proved that his gamble was paying off.

They drove out from the stable yard to start their deliveries. Josh smiled at Manuel, who looked up and grinned at his new mercantile store sign. He'd had it made to go up in front of the store. Manuel was exceedingly proud that he and Eliza now owned a mercantile store.

Josh smiled at him, but he understood how hard Manuel and Eliza had worked since they bought the general store. Manuel had reason to be proud of his success. This land encouraged hard work and enterprise, Josh was realising. If you tried your hardest and ignored the constant setbacks that the land itself, the weather, and the common problems that frontier life flung at every new homesteader and new business, the rewards could be substantial.

The day passed quickly for Josh and Manuel. The deliveries were speedily done, except for the visit to the Grangers. But neither Josh nor Manuel complained about that! Coffee laced with whisky, and another delicious cake made by Mrs Granger, made that visit not only enjoyable but essential to the success and enjoyment of the day's deliveries.

When they arrived back home, Manuel rushed into the store, eager to check that Eliza and Dora had faced no problems with the miners. Josh stabled the horse and followed Manuel into the store.

Eliza could hardly get the words out in her excitement.

They tumbled out as she told of the latest prophecies from the man who called himself Jeremiah.

"We'd no more visits from miners or prospectors today. Just the usual townspeople, all eager to discuss the latest fire and painted warnings after Jeremiah's prophecy. They say Jeremiah is going to come in to town on Sunday. He is going to preach a proper gospel and deliver yet more prophecies. Jeremiah is constantly talking about Sheriff Grey and how he is an evil man serving the Antichrist. The sermon and service Sheriff Grey holds in the saloon, Jeremiah has called an abomination. He says that the Lord will show his anger towards Preacher Grey."

Dora, standing beside her, was chewing her usual wad of tobacco and nodding her head. "Jeremiah is evil, masquerading behind twisted words of prophecy. This is going to lead to trouble on Sunday. I don't see Sheriff Grey standing by and taking these insults lightly." She spat out her wad of tobacco into the spittoon and gave her usual loud cackle of laughter. "I've never been to the services in the saloon on Sunday. But I sure am going to the one this Sunday. I wouldn't miss it. I reckon there's going to be fireworks when that Jeremiah takes on our preaching sheriff!"

CHAPTER FIFTY-ONE

Josh left the general store earlier than expected. Manuel told him to leave as soon as they were organized, after the last of the delivery boxes had been sorted out. Mrs Granger always gave them a couple of large cakes. Today it had been three, including a coffee cake. In return, Mr Granger received alcohol: sometimes beer, sometimes whiskey. Manuel and Josh left Mr Granger looked extremely happy, clutching his whiskey bottles.

Two other properties, which were owned by the Hobbs brothers, always had produce to exchange for some of their weekly provisions. Today, Manuel had returned with some smoked hams and tomatoes. One brother had an enclosed garden in which he grew many unusual crops, despite the changeable weather and the different seasons.

"Those Hobbs brothers produce wonderful smoked products. I wish I could get more from them," said Manuel. "Josh, why don't you take one cake, and I'll slice you some of the ham? I'm sure you'll manage that in your saddlebag."

Josh felt certain, in fact there was no doubt in his mind at all, that the cake and the delicious ham slices would be in his saddlebag, even if they got a bit squashed. Earlier that afternoon, he'd arranged to pick up a horse from the livery stable. He liked Reuben, the blacksmith, a large man with a barrel chest and gigantic biceps, and a sweet smile. No one knew why he and Sheriff Grey were at loggerheads; no one knew how the original argument had started. Josh was of the opinion that the two combatants could not remember either. But it was a matter of principle now. In the West, no one liked to lose face or be seen to back down from an argument. So, the stalemate continued: Reuben continued to refuse to make the metal cell bars for the jail; Sheriff Grey refused all offers of wooden shutters, wooden bars, and even ornate wooden carvings across the open window.

The horse Josh been given was a plodder. He plodded all the way down to the general store, and Josh foresaw a lengthy journey back to Dry Creek Ranch. Laden down, the horse didn't seem to mind the extra load, which included some of the badly bruised fruit and vegetables from the early morning miners' battle, cake, ham, and a couple of bottles of beer for Nat and Bill.

Eliza had rushed up to Josh and handed them to him. "It's their favourite one. We can't often get it from Seth, but tell them it's to cheer them up from me and Manuel, after the fire at their cabin."

Josh trotted along, thinking of how kind and generous Manuel and Eliza could be. The thought of saving the two veterans' favourite beer had been unexpected and heartwarming. Josh had to admit, though: he wished she'd added an extra bottle for himself. But, if he was honest, he really preferred a strong cup of coffee.

As he approached the Dry Creek Ranch, he could see the figures on the porch. At first, he could see they were ready for any attack and how they stood watching and waiting for his approach, to finally see if he was an enemy or not. He raised a hand and waved it at them, hoping they'd realize who he was. He'd told them, before he left, to be prepared to shoot on sight. It would not be funny if *he* was the first person they shot at!

"It's Josh!" A smile crossed Josh's face at the shout from Bill. They realized, when Bill was staying at Broken Horseshoe Ranch, that the man had an amazing long-distance sight. Josh relaxed and, without thinking, urged his horse to move faster. The plodding at the same steady pace continued and Josh resigned himself to arriving at Dry Creek Ranch whenever his horse felt like it.

"Did you have any visitors?" Josh shouted as he came nearer.

"No, it's been quiet," said Amy. "What about you? Nat said he left you in the middle of a fight on Main Street."

The plodding horse was safely stabled and fed and watered. Josh joined the others at the ranch house. Spread out on the table in the centre of the room were the accounts that Amy had been working on.

Josh walked in, carrying his parcels. "I hope this is all right: I brought some provisions back with me. Unfortunately, I think they may be squashed." He opened one saddlebag and produce the two bottles of beer, which he handed to Bill and Nat with an explanation. He only wished that Eliza could have seen the delight on their faces at this unexpected, and kind, gift.

"Now, this is the cake Mrs Granger made. I hope it's all right." Josh gingerly eased it out of its bag.

"Is it one of her coffee cakes?" Amy asked Josh eagerly. Turning to Hannah, she explained, "Mrs Granger is a most wonderful baker—her cakes are so delicious, but the coffee cake is best of all."

"It's just a plain jam sponge cake. She makes the jam with the fruit from her garden, and it tastes delicious," said Josh, finally retrieving the cake, which, to his relief, was only squashed on one side.

"There has been one unexpected development since you left Josh," said Bill. His beer was half finished, and he was trying to make it last longer by taking small sips in between mouthfuls of sponge cake.

"We don't quite know what to make of it," said Amy.

"It was Bill that found them. He better explain it all to you."

"Out around the barn, near the water trough, and around the ripest fruit and vegetables, I found small footprints. It looks as if someone has been eating the ripe fruit and vegetables and been wandering around the water trough. There's someone skulking about the ranch, someone tiny. I don't think it's got anything to do with Jeremiah. But we have to be on the lookout to see who it is and try to capture them tonight."

It was agreed. Between them, they would keep watch for the small intruder. They were puzzled that such a small footprint had been found on its own. No larger footprints had been found. Why was a child on their own? Why were they hiding?

CHAPTER FIFTY-TWO

While Josh was away in Nowhere doing store deliveries and working with Manuel, they had already started building a new cabin for Bill and Nat. Nancy had paid them a brief visit that morning. She brought with her some old timber and a few spare cooking utensils, even an old wonky table that had been in the horse's stable. Although it was a small amount to start with, both Bill and Nat were overjoyed.

"Maybe that Jeremiah did us a favour, Bill," Nat said as they began pacing out the foundations of the cabin. They had moved the new site of the cabin to a more sheltered position, one that was nearer the creek when it was actually flowing.

Josh was surprised to see that Hannah looked so much better on his return to the ranch. Josh then realized that the older woman had Amy and David with her. Hannah was enjoying the company of both Amy and her grandson. They had revitalized the older woman and he could see a difference in her already. No longer was she looking like an Apache in dress and demeanour. The characteristics of the girl she must have been when she was captured were becoming more evident every day. But everyone saw, by the way she kept looking out to the horizon, that she wouldn't rest or recover entirely until Sam and Matthew had returned safely at the ranch.

Amy and Hannah looked at the cake, and smiled at each other. Amy left Hannah to slice it. There would be little left of it: it was a rare treat to be enjoyed with a coffee.

"I think David should only have a small piece of cake. It looks delicious but is very rich for a young baby."

Hannah looked at Amy as she continued to cut up the cake into slices and continued speaking with a surprised look on her face. "Do you know, Amy, I can still remember how to bake a cake!"

Hannah reached out a finger and pushed a small piece of cake on her plate around, looking at it as if remembering past days and past cakes.

Josh, who was standing at the doorway, watched Hannah.

Catching sight of Josh, Hannah turned towards both of them and said in a quiet voice, "I haven't had cake in so many years. It was the last time we sat down as a family to have a meal. My mother made two large cakes the night before we left on the wagon train. It was our last night in our own home. Everything was out, ready for packing. I stood watching my mother bake those cakes. I remember helping her with the weighing in of the flour and sugar before packing them away in the wagon, ready for our morning departure." Hannah sat silent and still for a moment, fingering those pieces of cake crumbs, and the tears slowly rolled down her face.

Amy rushed to Hannah's side and put an arm round her. "It's all right, Hannah—you can cry, we'll understand."

Josh stood helplessly as he watched the two women and made to leave the cabin. He pushed open the door, but Amy stopped him.

"No, Josh, it's all right. You should eat. We've already had our meal, and you must be hungry. Hannah is fine. It's good that she can feel that she can talk about what's happened in her past and even shed a little tear. I don't expect you did before ..." Amy's voice trailed off. She could not comprehend all that this woman suffered, and yet Hannah had come through it all without a complete breakdown.

Hannah wiped the last tear away and gave them both a watery smile. "Amy is right. I *have* kept everything tucked away in the back of my mind. I knew a girl who cried all the time but it didn't help her. Early on in my captivity, I learned just to live for the day. Get through that day and put all my memories in the back of my mind. That life had gone, and I had to live somehow through the new life. I did it a day at a time."

There was a sudden silence that greeted these remarks. Neither Josh nor Amy knew what to say. They understood the problems and the depth of despair Hannah must have gone through, but both felt that anything they said would be meaningless.

Hannah was the one to break the silence, swiftly pulling herself upright. She hugged Amy hard and patted Josh on the arm. "Enough of that. Thank you for listening to my memories, but I will not dwell on the past. I am going to enjoy my present time with all of you and my lovely grandson!"

CHAPTER FIFTY-THREE

Josh was ushered into a chair, and Hannah served up a meal for him. Amy took David, who was getting restless, out onto the porch. She brought him to where Bill and Nat were sorting through the timber from Broken Horseshoe Ranch and the other wood from Dry Creek Ranch. Amy looked doubtfully at the collection piled up, and wondered how it might make a habitable home for the two men. As they seemed so delighted with it, Amy thought that they must be able to work out what they wanted to do with it, in some weird manner she couldn't fathom.

"David is so restless tonight—I thought that if I walked round with him, he might fall asleep," said Amy. But David waved at the two men in excitement, watching them lift the timber and sort out suitable lengths. He found it all interesting.

"He doesn't look very sleepy," said Bill with a laugh.

At the deep-throated laugh from the man beside him, David gave a loud chuckle, and stretched out towards him.

"No, David, the men are busy. We're only going to hold them up from their work. Look, it's getting darker. They're hurrying to get their work finished. Then they'll go to sleep. Don't you want to go to sleep?"

The two men laughed at the pleading note in Amy's voice as she spoke to David. With a rueful smile towards them, she walked away, leaving them in peace.

Amy, carrying the child, walked around. David was slowly drifting off to sleep as she walked alongside the vegetable plot Rosita had planted. The Mexican woman, who had worked for Nancy, was skilled at gardening, and her productive plot showed her hard work and intuitive skill with plants. But Amy could see that Nat and Hannah had carried on Rosita's work: the garden was weed free and as flourishing as it had been under Rosita's care. Hannah had been determined to prove herself worthy of living at the ranch, and was eager to please Nancy. Amy, looking at the vegetables and fruit stretching out neatly in rows, could only think that Hannah had been successful.

The sun was almost gone, and Devil's Mountain glinted in the distance. Dry Creek Ranch was further away from the mountains and foothills than Broken Horseshoe Ranch, whose actual boundaries included the foothills themselves. Here the land was flatter and less hilly and, apart from the lack of water, was fertile and had a gentle rolling aspect to it.

"This place could be lovely," Amy whispered to the baby. "If only we could find more water for it, it would flourish, and it could be beautiful."

Ambling along, she looked back at the ranch house; some shimmering shift in the atmosphere made it look very different. Amy could see, in that moment, the ranch house itself was larger, with additional buildings to the side. In front of it was a new, larger porch, with many flowering plants. Some were twisting their way around the porch loggia itself, in colourful, flowering strands of blossom. The sound of laughter from inside the ranch reached her ears. A large, elderly dog lying on the porch had three puppies playing beside her. She looked a lot like Meg but with grizzled whiskers. In the corral behind the ranch house, Amy saw Bella, her horse. But this was a much older Bella.

On the porch itself, a woman stood—much like herself, but again older. A young boy stood beside her.

The blond curls and the impish smile reminded her of David. Beside him, with a hand in the woman's, was another smaller boy. And the woman held a child in a pretty dress, carrying her much like Amy was carrying David.

A voice called out her name. A man's voice, and it seemed familiar. Then it was gone. The voice called out to her again: "Amy, my love!" And then there was nothing.

Her vision blurred, and the shimmering scene in front of her vanished. Only in the deepening dusk the Dry Creek Ranch house was in front of her— and there were no flowers, no laughter, and no voice calling her name. Amy shivered.

What had happened? What had she seen?

CHAPTER FIFTY-FOUR

The moon rose above the jagged peaks of Devil's Mountain. Shadows of purple and midnight blue merged into the chasms and canyons that shrouded the hillsides. The moon lit up paths of glittering, brilliant white alongside the shadows.

Dry Creek Ranch bathed in the moon's light, leaving shadowy pools behind the barn and the ranch house itself. Amy found herself unable to sleep and had joined Josh out on the porch, as he kept his watch for the intruder.

"Not tired?" Josh whispered as she came out onto the porch.

"Yes, but I couldn't sleep. I don't know why," Amy whispered back as she settled beside him on the bench.

"I would have thought doing those accounts all day would have made you sleepy. Looking at all those numbers in all those lines would have made me drift off, even during the day." A soft chuckle drifted towards Amy, following Josh's remark.

Amy smiled at him but then realized that Josh wouldn't be able to see it. They were out of the direct light of the moon, and it was far too dark. "Yes, they can be very tiring. Sometimes I think I'm seeing double the figures on the page. But it's helped Hannah, and Nat and Bill, with me being here on the ranch with them."

"I never knew you to be worried before when you stayed out here. What's making you so nervous? Is it Jeremiah and his prophecies?" Josh asked Amy.

There was silence for a moment. Josh felt Amy move restlessly beside him on the bench, almost as if she was thinking what to say. Then he felt her settle back against the rough wooden wall of the ranch house.

"It's hard to put into words, Josh. Yes, Jeremiah and his threats do worry me. But that's not all that's worrying me. There's an uneasiness hanging about the ranch. It's a feeling I have. There are those threats from Jeremiah but I also have a feeling of being watched by someone. It's not a good feeling. Someone is out there—watching us, taking note of our daily life. Almost as if they are becoming prepared for ..." Amy's voice trailed off, her whisper fading into the night.

For a long while, Josh said nothing. Amy did not exaggerate. She did not take fright at the slightest thing. If Amy felt uneasy and was worried about the possibility of danger coming to the inhabitants of Dry Creek Ranch, Josh believed her. With a start, Josh realized he had not spoken in reply to Amy. Choosing his words with care, he spoke with deliberation: "If you feel this uneasiness, I think we should take further precautions. I have faith in your gut feelings, Amy. They have served us well up in the mountains on our Jesuit treasure hunts. You must always tell me if you have these uneasy warning feelings."

"But what if I'm wrong? I may be mistaken. What then? We'll have taken precautions for nothing," said Amy.

"I don't care if you're wrong. I'd rather act and be safe. What if you're right, and we didn't bother? Tomorrow morning, we'll discuss it with the others and put a plan into place."

"If only Sam and Matthew would get home. It would make us more secure, with the extra firepower," Amy said.

Josh tried to look at Amy, but there was little to be seen in the shadows. He wondered how she really felt about Sam, and if she knew Sam was in love with her. Josh wondered how *he* felt about it himself, and how he would feel if Sam declared himself to Amy. But he thought it unlikely. Sam felt his mixed heritage was a problem and would not, Josh felt, have the confidence to speak to Amy.

Josh's thoughts were rambling around his brain when Amy clutched his arm. "There, over there! I saw a shadow flit across in front of the stable." Her words barely reached his ears. She had whispered softly, so as not to be heard by the intruder.

Amy and Josh rose to their feet and, silently, both moved towards the stable. Josh gestured to Amy to go to the right and he would move to the left, hoping to cut off any escape from the stable itself.

Josh thought the intruder must have been going to spend the rest of the night in the warmth of the stable amongst the straw and the horses. They had found no one present that morning, so their stay must only have been for a short while before dawn. He saw that Amy had reached one side of the stable wall. She paused, looking at him, and he could see in the growing light of the moon as it slid across in front of the stable that Amy had her gun out ready.

The stable door would never close properly; it was always slightly ajar. That had never been a problem—not until Jeremiah's prophecy and now this intruder. Only that morning, Bill said it was a chore he would tackle later that day. But after Nancy's arrival with the timber, both he and Nat had been too eager to begin work on their cabin, and the faulty stable door had been forgotten.

"Let me go in first," whispered Josh. "I'll fling the door open wide, and you come in on my right."

Moonlight had by now reached them, and they both could see each other clearly. The darkness within the stable itself was daunting. Both of them wondered how this intruder would react to their sudden appearance.

Amy nodded at Josh. "Ready," she whispered.

Josh took a deep breath, raised his gun in one hand and with the other gripped the side of the stable door. Without looking at Amy, he was conscious of her stiffening beside him. Also taking a deep breath, Amy had her gun raised, ready to fire if necessary.

Josh pulled the door back. He shouted as he leapt through the stable door.

"Now!"

CHAPTER FIFTY-FIVE

The stable door hurtled open with a loud squeak and crash. Moonlight flooded in behind Josh and Amy. The whole of the stable was lit up as bright as day.

"It's a small boy!" Amy whispered and put the gun away in her pocket.

The smell of the stable was overpowering once the door was open. But the scent of the horses—and the hay and straw—was a comforting aroma. Made of adobe and rough-hewn wood, it had sheltered horses on the Dry Creek Ranch since the first settlers arrived there. Nancy had often said it had been built first as the horses had been a priority for the early owners of the ranch.

Beside Amy, Josh carefully put his gun in its holster as he stood staring at the young child. Huddled in the corner stable, the child sat with his knees drawn up to his chest. His eyes were wide as he looked up in terror at the two figures, shadowy with the moon flooding in behind them.

Amy thought they must have looked terrifying to the child. The moon shining behind them meant they were both she and Josh were in dark shadow. No wonder the child was frightened, Amy thought, and stepped forward, putting out her hand.

"Don't be frightened. We won't hurt you," Amy said and took another step forward, but she stopped as the child whimpered at her progress towards it. With a sudden movement, it drew back into the safety of its corner.

The door of the Dry Creek Ranch house was flung open. "Josh? Amy? Where are you? Are you both all right?" Hannah shouted out, and she and the men rushed down to the stable. They had heard Josh's shout as he flung open the stable door. They all thundered towards the stable door, guns ready for action.

They reached the stable door and stood for a moment. The moonlight showed them all the situation inside the stable with the child. Gathering together behind Josh and Amy, there was a sudden silence. Amy smiled to herself as all the guns were quickly hidden away. The child moved slightly and gave another whimper of fear.

"Oh, my! What are you doing here? Why are you on your own? What's happened to the family?" Hannah gave out a loud cry and rushed forward to the child. She spoke rapidly, all her words now in the Indian language she had learned whilst in captivity. Kneeling down in front of the child, she put out her arms. With a sudden cry of recognition, the child flung itself into Hannah's arms, sobbing hysterically.

The men drifted away. This was not a good time to crowd around the frightened, sobbing child.

Josh looked at Amy. "What should we do?" he asked her. His words were heard by Hannah, who stood up and, taking the child's hand, walked towards Josh and Amy.

"Hot water, Josh, please. The child is filthy."

Josh nodded and turned go back up to the ranch house. "We need a fresh pot of coffee as well," Amy heard him mutter under his breath.

Amy looked at the child, and then at Hannah. "I'll get some clothes ready for ..." Her voice drifted away as she looked again as Hannah approached her, her arm around the shoulders of the young child.

"This is ..." Hannah looked down at the little boy, then shook her head. "I can't translate it to English, Amy. It's a mixture of flowers, all together in one phrase—in the Apache language."

By this time they had reached the porch, where the men had gathered. Bill was seated on the bench, whilst the others sat on the porch itself or stood leaning against the rail.

It was Bill who spoke: "I think that could translate easily to Flora." The obvious learning of the former professor was coming out. He looked even more closely at the child, who was standing there clad in dirty buckskin breeches and a heavy cotton shirt. The short hair straggled around the small, pinched face: a very dirty face, stained from the stolen fruit and plastered with dust and dirt. "But isn't the child a boy? I can't think of a boy's name to split that phrase into."

CHAPTER FIFTY-SIX

Hannah looked at the child and spoke again in the Indian language. The child clutched her hand and began sobbing. Between sobs, the words poured out in a garbled torrent of anguish. The face of Hannah tightened into a mask of worry and horror at the child's words.

Hannah stooped again, this time clasping the child in a tight, comforting grip. Looking around at the concerned faces, she spoke over the child's shoulder: "This is a girl. She was with her family. They were my husband's brother, wife, and children. We all hid together up in the ancient cave dwellings. You remember seeing them, Josh and Amy, don't you?"

Josh answered Hannah's question: "Yes, you all came down out of the old ruined village high on the cliff face. We watched you before you parted company. They went off towards the river, whilst you made your way down the canyon. That was where we met up with you after you were ambushed." Remembrance of the event, during which Amy's knife skills had saved them all from the hidden assassin's gun, passed through his mind.

Hannah continued speaking: "They were going to make their way to the new tribal reservation and join the rest of their family, who had gone on ahead. But they realized it was dangerous travelling, so the girl became a boy. They had got only a short way from where Sam and I, and Matthew, met up with both of you. When they saw some men coming to attack them, her mother pushed the child down into a gully as they fled." Hannah paused, and her grip tightened on the still crying child. "Her mother called to her to track us and find safety with me and Sam."

"What happened to the rest of the family?" Josh asked, fearing the answer.

Hannah's face hardened, and she put a protective hand on the child's head. Thankful that her words would not be understood by the girl, she began speaking: "They were captured, tied together in a long line, and marched off. None of them were killed or even injured. She climbed out of the gully and followed our tracks to the ranch. It's amazing that the hard journey to Dry Creek Ranch here was managed by such a young child,"

"Let's bathe her and give her something to eat," Amy said, ever the practical one.

Hannah smiled at Bill as she bent down again to give the child a hug. "Bill, your name was just right. Flora will do nicely, with Flora actually being a girl. Her mother thought it best she looked like a boy travelling, so the wonderfully long braids she had were cut off."

Gently, Hannah pushed the child away from her and pointed to the people standing around. They smiled at the child, trying to reassure her. All of them wanted her to realize that she was no longer in danger and was being cared for by friendly folk.

The sudden wail from a bedroom shattered the night: David was awake and wanted everyone to know it. The girl's eyes widened, and she spoke rapidly to Hannah. A smile lit up Hannah's face as she laughed with the girl. "Yes, it's David!"

Amy had rushed in to the baby and lifted him up. His angry wails ceased abruptly when he saw her. She lifted him up. Grabbing a braid, he stuck the end in his mouth and began chewing. Amy brought him out onto the porch, where they all were still gathered.

Flora gave a great cry of joy. "David!" The Apache

girl ran forward but stopped and looked anxiously towards the baby boy. Then, a torrent of words tumbled out of her mouth as she spoke to Hannah, who was standing beside her.

Amy came forward with David. She sat on the bench on the porch, settling the baby on her knee. With one hand, she patted the space beside her. "Flora, come and sit beside me."

Hannah placed an arm around the child and pushed her gently towards the bench as she spoke softly to her in the Indian language. Then Hannah turned and spoke to Amy. "Flora remembers David being born. We were in a close-knit community and often Flora would look after David for my daughter."

Josh thought back to the horrific murder of David's parents. Both he and Amy had discovered them killed by bandits. David's mother had hidden the baby before they had finally caught up and killed her. It was Amy who, with the help of Leah at Broken Horseshoe Ranch, had nursed the baby through the difficult early months of his time with them.

The attack on the family and the sight of them being marched off as prisoners had been a horrifying spectacle for Flora to witness. How she had managed to climb out of the gully that her mother had pushed her down for safety, and then track them back to Dry Creek Ranch, was astonishing.

Hannah, and her reassuring, warm presence, had done much to ease the suffering and fear of the young girl. But Amy could see the wistful look in Flora's eyes as she stared down at the wriggling baby in her arms. Was she remembering better times with the baby and her family? The long braids she had worn had been shorn, and she was clad in the outfit of a young Apache boy. She looked very different from the girl that had looked after him in the Indian encampment. He had been such a tiny baby when she had looked after him. Flora was given a gentle push by Hannah, and she slowly approached David. It was doubtful that he would remember her.

CHAPTER FIFTY-SEVEN

Hannah, Bill, and Nat stood around Josh and Amy as they both sat at the table, finishing their breakfast.

Bill was the one who spoke: "We will be fine. We are all armed. The main porch on the ranch overlooks all approaches to the ranch house itself. Both of you are expected at the general store. You can't keep missing it. Broken Horseshoe Ranch relies on your work at the store for all its food and general provisions. Manuel could easily replace both of you if you keep missing days."

Josh finished his cup of coffee. He set it down on the table and looked across at Amy. "What do you think? You finished all the accounts yesterday, didn't you?"

Amy twisted her braid around between her fingers, her snub nose wrinkling in distaste at how soggy it was. David woke up early and Amy tried to calm him down by nursing him, and he'd grabbed the braid from her before she could remove it from his chubby hand. "They are right. If we lose our jobs, Broken Horseshoe Ranch wouldn't survive. No, Josh, we must keep going to work and taking in the produce that's grown here on this ranch as well. It's a tough life out here, and we must ensure some outside income, because neither ranch is self-sufficient."

Josh stood. He pushed his chair back in and looked round at the others. "All right, but you must promise us one thing: all of you must stay close to the ranch house. Keep a sharp lookout and be prepared for an attack of any kind."

Sometime later, Josh and Amy sat on their horses and looked at the porch before they left Dry Creek Ranch. Ranged along the porch were Hannah, who had David in her arms and Flora standing beside her, holding her hand. Alongside them, Nat stood with his rifle, and Bill had his weapon at the ready.

"Goodbye, both of you! Take care on the journey!" Bill chuckled at his remark, hinting that they may be as much at risk as those living on the ranch.

They had travelled some miles before Amy spoke. "What a difference in Flora this morning. Washed, dressed in a cutdown blouse of mine, a good night's sleep and some proper food, and she looked a different girl."

"She was a plucky girl. I'm amazed that she tracked us all the way to the ranch. For such a youngster, that shows some skill in tracking. Having Hannah, someone she knows and is familiar with, has helped enormously. But what worries me is what happened to her family."

"Do you think they were going to kill them? Why else would the men tie them together and march them off? Maybe Flora didn't see it properly? She was down in that gully. She may have been mistaken," Amy said, trying to think things through from the limited information that they had gleaned from the girl's tale.

Josh lifted his hand with his forefinger and pushed his hat to the back of his head. Amy could see that he was obviously thinking hard. "That young girl is bright. No way would she be mistaken in what she saw. If she says they were all roped together and marched off in a long line, that's what happened. What beats me is, why? Why not shoot them on the spot? I don't understand why they did that."

Neither of them could make sense of the men's actions at all, and both gradually drifted into a companionable silence as they rode towards Nowhere.

Unpacking the last of the vegetables from Dry Creek

Ranch, Amy handed the empty box back to Josh and spoke to him with surprise in her voice: "I'm pleased to be back in Nowhere. Don't get me wrong, Josh—I love living on the ranch. But it's good to get back in here, to see Eliza, and to hear what's been going on in the town itself."

Amy had greeted Eliza and baby Isabel on her arrival. After she had given the completed accounts to the delighted Manuel, she was now on her way to the saloon to give Seth his account books.

Standing outside the swing doors, Amy took a deep breath. She didn't like going into the saloon. But it was early morning, so she reckoned it wouldn't be too busy. Later in the afternoon and evening, after much drinking, the crowd of men grew noisy and belligerent. Fights broke out for no apparent reason; punches were thrown, and tables got smashed on almost a nightly basis. Amy pushed open the swing doors and stood for a moment, looking around the room. The smell of stale beer and smoke from the night before was strong. There were only a few old-timers seated at the bar. For all Amy knew, they had been there from the night before. She remained for a moment in the doorway.

"Amy! Over here, girl. Join me at the bar, whilst I get ready for the evening session." Seth raised a welcoming hand, gesturing Amy towards him. She could see that he was stocking the bar with bottles and sorting out glasses. "Can I offer you a drink, girl?"

"No thanks, Seth—I've brought you the finished accounts," said Amy. She placed the completed books on the top of the bar counter and pushed them towards the man standing behind it.

Seth wiped his hands on a towel he'd tucked into the

apron he wore. Checking they were clean and dry, he opened one book, and then the other. For a long moment, he stared at them both, then a slow smile crossed his face. "Well, girl, that Manuel was right all along. You *have* done wonders on these books. I can see at a glance what's happening. I reckon you deserve payment for this. Worth every penny." Seth reached down under the counter and produced a bag of coins, which he handed to her. "Just as promised, but with an added extra for your Pa. I know this is his favourite." Again, he reached down under the counter, this time producing a large bottle of whiskey, which he pushed across the counter towards her.

Amy's eyes widened. "That really is my Pa's favourite whiskey. Thank you, Seth. He'll love this."

After discussing how often Amy would pick up the books and do her magic on them, she left with a broad smile on her face. The little bag in her pocket was jingling happily and the bottle of whiskey clutched tightly to her chest. Not only was she doing the books for the saloon and the general store but Seth had also told her the hotel keeper wanted her help with his books too. Amy was looking forward to visiting the hotel later that day to sort out the conditions and payment she would receive for doing the hotel books.

Amy would not have been so keen to visit the hotel if she had known in advance what awaited her there!

CHAPTER FIFTY-EIGHT

On returning to the general store, Amy was surprised to see Tom had arrived and was talking to the others. He turned and smiled at her. "I know it's not the day to come in for provisions, but your Pa wanted me to come in because he knew you'd be working today. He wants you both to go back to Broken Horseshoe Ranch this evening. He's found some signs that he wants you both to look at."

"Tom! It's so good to see you." Amy rushed up to the young Chinese boy and gave him a hug. His grin was wide across his face as he hugged her back. Amy had only been a short time at Dry Creek Ranch and was surprised at how much she missed the company of the Broken Horseshoe Ranch family.

"We'll take the buggy back to Broken Horseshoe Ranch, and Tom will go to Dry Creek Ranch with their provisions. Then he'll return to the ranch by horse," Josh explained to Amy.

"Your Pa is missing you both. The place seems quiet without you and the baby," Tom said as he began filling a canvas sack with the provisions Chan had requested.

"Look, Dora and I are here to help Eliza. It's been slow today, not many folks around. Why don't you three set off home while it's still light?" Manuel suggested to them.

Tom finished packing the provisions for the Broken Horseshoe Ranch and took the boxes out to the buggy to take back. Meanwhile, Josh began filling in the list that Nat had given him for Dry Creek Ranch. Tom was going back to Dry Creek with the provisions before returning to Broken Horseshoe Ranch.

Amy went in to the back bedroom to kiss Isabel

goodbye. She exchanged hugs with Eliza and Dora. Then she set out for the hotel to discuss her work with the owner and collect his account books.

After the death of the previous owner, who had been shot by the sheriff, the hotel had been sold to a man coming from somewhere back east. His visits had been sporadic, and no one knew the man apart from having the occasional brief conversation with him. Whilst he had been absent from the hotel, it had been run by an elderly bartender who, whilst managing the day-to-day routine of the hotel and bar in a slipshod fashion, completely neglected the hotel account books.

Manuel praised Amy to Seth who ran the saloon, so gaining her saloon account books to work on. Seth, in turn, told the hotel owner, who was eager to find someone to take the nitpicking task of sorting through the hotel's accounts off his hands. He was eager to hire her.

Amy walked up the dusty main street of Nowhere. She paused to speak to a couple of women, both out to shop at the general store and looking for someone to gossip with. But Manuel had been correct: the town was quiet. The miners were nowhere to be seen, all busy prospecting in the foothills of Devil's Mountain for more gold or silver. She walked past the saloon. The swing doors were closed, but the noisy chatter and laughter of the few customers could be heard. The clink of glasses drifted out towards her, along with the ever-powerful stench of the beer.

Wrinkling her nose at the smell, she walked on towards the hotel. Amy hadn't been in it for some time— not since the shootout between the former hotel owner and the sheriff. Amy grimaced; that had not been a pleasant experience. She was about to step up onto the boardwalk and go into the hotel itself when a voice halted her progress.

"Miss Amy! I haven't seen you for some days. How are you? Still as lovely as ever, I see!" The flattering, smarmy voice of Charles Roberts came to her as he walked out of the livery stables. "I was called away on business. I wonder if you missed seeing me around Nowhere?" He walked towards the girl, his eyes roving unpleasantly over her slim form. Despite the dust from his journey on his horse, Charles was still dressed impeccably as ever. The expensive jacket was cut perfectly to fit his large, fleshy frame. As always, he wore a vest of intricate design in a colourful fabric. Against her will, Amy's eyes were drawn to that vest, and she was conscious of his gloating smile as she followed the path of the embroidered bluebirds over his chest.

"Good afternoon, Mr Roberts. I hope you had a successful business trip," Amy replied, trying to ignore the way her flesh crawled at his gaze. She was clad, as always, in her buckskin jacket, the canvas skirt she wore today, had, as usual, the two huge pockets. Each pocket contained a weapon, her knife in one, and her Colt in the other pocket. Her only feminine quirk was the bandanas she always wore—each one a bright colour, often red— and sometimes she wore a matching red hat. Slung across her body, or over her shoulder, was a canvas satchel that held items Amy thought essential for frontier life.

"Why so formal, Miss Amy? I've told you so many times, please call me Charles," he said as he drew nearer to her.

Amy smiled at him, but not a very big smile: a weak, watery, polite smile. But she felt that Charles Roberts needed to be kept sweet. She loathed him and inexplicably feared him. Provoking the man served no purpose. Both she and Josh reckoned *he* knew who wanted Josh dead and who had paid for the abortive attempts on Josh's life. Amy put on speed to get into the hotel as quickly as possible so that she could cut short her conversation with Charles Roberts.

"I must go into the hotel, Mr ... er ... Charles, if you'll excuse me," Amy replied.

His eyebrows were raised quizzically at this, but Amy said no more. She walked across the boardwalk and pushed open the hotel door. Amy walked through it and into the lobby. For a moment, she could only stand still—and then she screamed.

CHAPTER FIFTY-NINE

Sprawled across the lobby floor was the hotel owner. Blood had oozed out from his head, and formed a pool around him. Amy stood transfixed in horror. Used to sudden death, even sometimes being the cause of the actual death, Amy had thought she was immune to the sight of bloodshed and sudden death. Somehow, the sheer unexpected reality of the murdered man in front of her had shaken her. She backed away from the body. It was pointless to check if he was alive. No one could survive that ghastly wound in the back of his head. Scrambling behind her, she somehow managed to thrust the door back open, and emerged into the bright sunlight of the afternoon in Nowhere.

"Help! Someone—come and help!" Amy shouted. The hotel itself stood proudly on Main Street. Originally a wooden structure at the front, with the tent bedrooms behind, it had housed beds in rows and a large table and kitchen. The previous owner built on to the wooden frontage and it now boasted a dining room, kitchen, and bedrooms, all made of wood. There had been talk of the new hotel owner's grandiose plans to build a second storey, or even demolish the present building and start again.

Whatever plans the owner had imagined for the future of the hotel, Amy thought, would be gone forever. She shouted yet again and this time was thankful to see the sheriff emerge from his office further up the hill and run down towards her.

Charles Roberts was the one who reached her first. Despising the man, especially his flattering remarks towards her, Amy was nevertheless delighted when he ran towards her. "What's wrong Amy? Are you hurt?" Charles asked her.

"No—in there, in the lobby. He's dead." Amy stood back and pointed through the half-open door of the hotel entrance. Charles pushed the door open wide, stood there for a moment, and looked back at her, and at the sheriff, who had reached them both.

"He's dead all right. Someone made sure of it," Charles said.

"What are you doing here, Amy?" the sheriff asked her, surprised to see her there. Every woman who entered the hotel either had a companion or stayed overnight.

"The owner asked if I would sort out his account books. He told Seth at the saloon that they were in a muddle and I was to collect them today. They would be left in the front lobby, along with payment for me." As Amy spoke, she looked around the small entrance lobby of the hotel. A narrow desk was placed along the side of the lobby. There was a large guest book, obviously meant to impress guests when they signed in. A box—brimming with a mix of receipts, notes, and itemized bills—sat beside the book. Tucked in at the side was a small canvas bag. A scribbled note said in large letters, *Miss Amy*. Amy pointed to the box and the note on top of it. "That must be for me," she said.

Amy now sat in the general store, the others clustered around her, listening to her tell of the death of the hotel keeper. There was a general air of puzzlement amongst everyone. No one had actually known the man; he had just appeared in Nowhere on fleeting visits.

Josh had taken the box from Amy and was flicking through the various pieces of paper and receipts. He was wondering if a clue could be amongst them, giving a reason for the man's death. But nothing leapt out during his search.

The door of the general store opened, and Sheriff Grey walked in with a worried face. "That's good. You two haven't left for the Broken Horseshoe Ranch yet. I hoped I might catch you both."

For the first time since Josh had known the sheriff, he saw that the man was at a loss as to how to proceed. He shifted his feet and looked at Josh, swallowed a couple of times, and then took a deep breath. The silence in the general store had grown and was now heavy with apprehension. It was clear to everyone that Sheriff Grey had nothing pleasant to share with them. That expression on his face was not good. Observing the older man's determined expression, Josh understood it spelled trouble for him alone.

"No easy way of saying this, Josh. Don't like to be the bearer of bad news and don't understand this at all. But I must get to the actual point of why am here." The tall man, clad as usual all in black, rested his hands on his gun belt, and swayed backwards and forwards on the balls of his feet. "It concerns you, Josh."

CHAPTER SIXTY

Josh could see the man's jaw flex and set hard before he finally looked directly at Josh and spoke. "Not going to beat about the bush, Josh. But the dead man up there in the hotel was mistaken for you!"

Exclamations of dismay, horror, and surprise came from every one of them. Both Josh and Amy noticeably paled at this news, and Amy sank down onto a chair.

"How was the hotel owner mistaken for me?" Josh asked the sheriff. He was proud of himself. His voice, when asking the question, didn't waver or show any deep concern. "We don't look alike, I ..." Josh's voice faded away as he tried to understand how the killer could make the mistake.

Sheriff Grey looked sympathetically at Josh and took a deep breath before continuing.

"That dead man held in his hand a letter meant for you. It had your name on it, and he was obviously standing in the lobby reading it. There were other letters that he must have picked up from Duloe town before he arrived in Nowhere. Not only had he opened your letter but also a couple of other people's letters. Why he wanted to read everyone else's mail, I don't know. If he hadn't, he'd be alive now." In disgust, the sheriff slapped his thigh with his hand and shook his head. "Anyway, Josh, here's the letter for you." The piece of paper with Josh's name and Nowhere written in large letters was handed to Josh. He took it from the sheriff's hand, avoiding the bloodstained edges of it.

Manuel, eaten up with curiosity, tried to look over Josh's shoulder to read it. "Well, Josh? What does it say?" the storekeeper demanded of Josh.

"Nothing. There is nothing written on the inside of the paper. Why would anyone send me a letter, pay for it, and write nothing on it?" Josh's voice held all the mystification that he felt. "Why would anyone do this?" The name and address on one side of the paper was written in large bold capitals, whereas the folded inside of the paper was blank.

Sheriff Grey nodded and gave a sigh of satisfaction. "Just what I thought. Why send an empty letter to you? I don't understand it at all," Sheriff Grey said as he stood looking at Josh. "Well, the curiosity of George Binns was a death warrant for him. It was clutched in his hand and he was obviously reading it, or looking at it, when he was knocked down by a heavy blow to the head. Someone came up behind him, saw the name on the letter and acted. Killed outright, he was. One fatal blow to the head." The sheriff nodded to every one of them in turn, and spun round on his black embossed leather boots, and swept out of the door, those black coat tails of his long coat flying out behind him.

In the silence that followed the sheriff's departure, it was Manuel who clapped his hands in excitement. He looked straight at Josh. "The killer didn't know what you looked like, or where you would be. That letter was his way of identifying you. If he followed the letter, it would lead him directly to you. That must have seemed like a clever plan when he thought of it," Manuel said. He took the letter from Josh's fingers and was turning it over and over, hoping to find some clue on it, or some sign as to who had sent it to Josh. "Let's hope he's gone. He may never realize that he's killed the wrong man. If he left Nowhere immediately after killing the hotel keeper, he may still be in ignorance of who he actually murdered."

"Let's pray and hope so," Eliza said. Her hands were joined as if in prayer, and she was looking up, as if to heaven.

"Yes, let's hope so," agreed Amy.

Josh murmured his assent to these remarks, but his attention was on neither Amy nor Eliza. He was watching Dora. The large woman normally had plenty to say on every occasion Her silence was unusual, and the normally ruddy complexion had turned into an ashen colour. Standing somewhat apart from everybody, she was at the back of the store and, as Josh watched, she reached behind her for the chair that always stood there. So many of the ladies that came into the shop for their provisions also came in to chat over the events that had occurred in Nowhere and the surrounding area. The chair, often used for these occasions, had *never* been used by Dora. So, Josh was surprised and intrigued by the woman's apparent shock at the news of George Binns, the hotel keeper's death.

Should he walk over to her and ask what was wrong? He desperately wanted to, but Dora was an extremely private person. No one knew why she was in Nowhere; no one knew anything about her past. The tough lady with a shotgun kept everyone at a distance. Josh hesitated, then gave a speaking glance at Amy, nodding his head towards Dora. Amy understood his meaning and walked over to Dora, gently placing her hand on the shoulder of the older woman, who sat visibly stunned at the news of the hotel keeper's death.

"Dora, what's wrong? Don't you feel well? Dora, can I help you?"

CHAPTER SIXTY-ONE

Dora shook her head and stood up. She smoothed down the fabric of her skirt, her eyes fixed on a slight stain. "Oh, dear, I wonder what that mark is. Perhaps if I just sprinkle some water on it and wipe it away? I must do that at once. I don't want it to stain." Dora almost ran out of the door to the back of the store to reach the jug of water. All those left behind could only watch as she vanished through the door with a rustle of her black skirt.

Amy turned round to Josh and the others. "What was that all about? Was it something I said? I was only trying to help her, she looked so ill," Amy said, a puzzled look on her face.

Eliza stepped forward and gave Amy a hug. "No, it was nothing you said. The death of the hotel keeper has really upset her. Dora is a very private lady. In fact, you could say she's secretive about her past. I expect she will tell us all about it when she's ready. We must carry on and ignore this strange reaction of hers until she feels like talking about it," Eliza said.

Manuel was about to speak, but the door opened with a sudden rush.

Rueben, the blacksmith, stormed in, indignant at the prophet's latest activity. "It's Jeremiah! Would you believe it? He's been preaching at the Hobbs brothers' ranches, and now he's threatened them with fire and brimstone. All because they wouldn't kneel and pray. That was bad enough, but he's now demanding they give him a tenth of their income! They refused to give him anything. Jeremiah said that he is due to get tithes from them. When they argued with him, he began quoting from the Bible."

"Why would they pay him?" Manual asked Rueben, surprised at this strange demand from Jeremiah.

"He says that he is a man of God and therefore deserves payment. He quoted passages from the Bible to them. I can tell, you those Hobbs brothers were not happy with him. They warned him as he was leaving. That night they would keep watch, and if anyone trespassed on their land intending to burn buildings or painting words on walls, they would be shot." Rueben was delighted at the astonished reaction from everyone.

"They'll do it. The Hobbs brothers are quiet and soft-spoken—but they are not stupid. They know what he's up to, and they'll make certain that nothing on their land will be damaged tonight. I only hope he doesn't try anything with them," Manuel said. "They'll fight him."

"The Hobbs family never comes into town," Rueben said. "But I hear they're going to come in on this Sunday. The whole family is coming to support Sheriff Lance Grey when he holds the service in the saloon." Rueben laughed and looked around at them after getting the sacks of flour, sugar, and coffee he was shopping for. "Got no time for that man, Lance Grey. Had my disagreements with him, as you well know. But I would not miss that service on Sunday for anything." He paid Eliza and picked up his shopping. "Reckon it's going to be a good one. Hope Lance Grey's got a powerful sermon worked out. He's going to have plenty of people listening to him this Sunday."

The early start home to Broken Horseshoe Ranch was not so early, after all. The death of George Binns at the hotel, and the chat about Jeremiah with Rueben, had delayed them. So, it was nearly their usual time when Josh and Amy set off back to Broken Horseshoe Ranch.

Despite being tired, they were confident that the people waiting for them would be eager to hear the news and gossip. Once they heard about the hotel keeper's death, they wouldn't mind their late arrival.

It was a silent start to their journey back to the ranch. So much had happened that afternoon, and neither of them could think about it clearly. It was all so unexpected and puzzling. For Amy, the dead man's tragic end was still fresh in her mind, and she was finding it hard to move on from it.

"Do you really think that these attempts may be finished with? If this latest killer sends back information that I am dead, surely it is finally over?" Josh asked her, breaking the silence.

Alongside him, Amy thought for a while before answering him. Sadly, she shook her head. "I don't think so, Josh. We both think Charles Roberts is the informant of your whereabouts and activities to the evil man seeking your death. If we are correct, Charles will soon tell him that a mistake has been made. Then he will know that you are alive. But if we are mistaken, and Charles Roberts isn't an informant, you may well be safe now. I hope so."

The buggy trundled along for some time; the wheels, with their repetitive noise, and the jingle of the harness were the only sounds in the deepening twilight. The shadows of the Seguaro cacti became darker and longer, and the red stone cliffs of Devil's Mountains grew purple in their growing darkness.

"I think you're right, Amy. But yet another man has died in this endless vendetta against me." Josh raised his hand to stop Amy from speaking. He spoke again, this time with a harsh, dry laugh. "Don't worry—I won't run off as I threatened to do before. There's no future in that, as you have so often told me. He would only find me again, and then I would be without friends and allies. But Amy, I don't think we should just sit back and wait for the next attack."

Josh grew silent for a moment. Amy thought Josh didn't feel the despair that had engulfed him after the buggy had exploded behind the general store. This time she could see that a gathering determination now seemed to grow in him.

"Charles Roberts holds the key to the man behind my attacks. How about we search for that man? Charles Roberts thinks he's very clever. Perhaps, in his arrogant belief in his own superior abilities, we could find a weakness. Let's find out more about Charles Roberts, and maybe he will lead me to the man who is trying to kill me!"

CHAPTER SIXTY-TWO

The welcome that Josh and Amy received made their late arrival worthwhile. The meal Tom produced for them was superb and both made valiant efforts to eat everything that the young man had especially made for them. After Nat's basic cooking at Dry Creek, Tom's meals were like a banquet. A delicately flavoured chicken soup was followed by the actual chicken itself, along with rice and fresh-cut vegetables. The aroma had made Josh's mouth water before he'd even taken his seat.

"I want you both to go out with Ben and Chan to search this part of the property." Luke placed his map on the table and moving their plates to one side, despite them both still eating. His eagerness to follow up on the vague clues they had already found was so obvious.

Josh raised an eyebrow and looked towards Amy, who gave him a slight nod of agreement. Her father was overwhelmed with excitement, yet a hint of worry was in his voice. Amy was concerned that he was becoming too involved in the search. His health was precarious, and she thought it may well be too much for him.

Luke continued speaking. "One of the ranch hands from the Grangers' property came over yesterday morning with a message from Mr Granger to warn us about strangers. Seemingly, a young lad from a property further west has vanished. On an adjoining property, another couple of young lads have also disappeared. Ben always takes Meg with him. She barked furiously yesterday at a couple of rough guys who were watching them from a high ridge nearby."

Josh put his knife and fork down with a clatter on his plate. "Flora's family was taken off by a couple of men.

She saw them, and they were roped together. There was nothing we could do. We didn't know about it until we found Flora hiding around the Dry Creek barn" Luke continued speaking: "I don't like it. There is something going on, and I don't want these two young ones going out without a proper guard with them." Luke raised his hand at the protests from Ben and Chan. "I know you both are armed, but I will feel better if there is a larger group searching alongside you. The targeting of young men seems strange. But I don't want to risk anything happening to you both."

Ben subsided with a cross look on his face, but Chan was smiling happily. Josh saw that the young Chinese boy was happy that Luke considered him part of the family and cared about his safety.

Plans were made for an early start. Tom had a lunch bag half prepared, and would finish it in the morning at breakfast time. The tools needed for digging and exploring were placed out on the porch. Luke hovered over it all, his excitement only clouded because he couldn't go with them. His health had improved dramatically since he took the herbal medicine that Sam had got from an older Apache from the encampment. Much as he'd like to join the young ones on the actual physical investigation, Luke knew his capabilities. It had been hard to come to terms with his frailty. He had to realize that his increased fitness was not up to the journey or the physical digging required at the new site.

All was quiet, and Amy snuggled back down into her bed in her wallpapered cupboard bedroom. Those few nights away at Dry Creek Ranch had been enjoyable. Much as she loved being with Hannah, and getting to know her and exploring the ranch, it was good to get back home. The walls had been papered, by the previous owner of Broken Horseshoe Ranch, with the newspapers of the time. They were now familiar to Amy, and she greeted the faded photographs as if meeting up with old friends.

Before falling asleep, Josh's mind wandered over the plans they had made for the following day's investigation. He was now in a bunk bed in the purpose-built room that had been added to Broken Horseshoe Ranch by Nancy on her arrival. A marriage of convenience it may have been, but both Nancy and Luke had benefited from their marriage. Nancy had reorganized the ranch on her arrival, adding two more rooms. One was a bedroom for herself and another for Ben, Tom, Chan, and Josh. The bunk beds were capacious and were used by the four of them for the time being. Nancy's next project, with Tom's enthusiastic approval, was to be a new kitchen built alongside the ranch but separated by a porch way. It had been started then stopped for a while, but her enthusiasm for it had not diminished. Tom was so eager for it and insisted there would be room for him to sleep in it.

Tomorrow, they would have to be on their guard if the rumours about the missing ranch hands were true. Josh hoped that something of value would be found at this site. Ben had strongly insisted, along with Ezra, it was without a doubt a Jesuit site. Luke's enthusiasm was at fever pitch. Josh was worried that if nothing came of this the man could suffer a relapse in his health. Both he and Amy had been disappointed so many times. They had made light of the despair and futility they had felt over the constant search for Jesuit gold. Josh was wondering if that had been a mistake. Perhaps the disappointments should have been stressed. The few successful finds they had made were all that Luke could think of. He dismissed the many hours and the hardship on their journeys they had endured.

The nighttime sounds of the ranch were added to by the snoring and snuffling of the sleeping inhabitants. All except Josh. He couldn't sleep. Taking care not to wake the others, he crept out of the small bedroom, across the main living room of the ranch house, and out onto the porch. The night was cool, and the air was fresh with a slight breeze. He sat on the chair that was always used by Luke. Wrapping his blanket around him, Josh settled down in the chair, enjoying the comfort of it. Luke was in bed. He didn't need it. Josh knew why he was awake: the death of George Binns was preying on his mind.

"If only I could remember! Why can't I? What did I do that made someone so eager to find me and kill me? Again and again, he's sent others to kill me. I will not sit back any more. I'm going to find him and find out what exactly he has against me." Those murmured words, with the resolution behind them, calmed Josh, and he drifted off to sleep.

The jingle of harness and the trundling noise of the buggy approaching the ranch jerked him awake. Automatically, he felt for his gun. He didn't have it— he'd left it inside. And the buggy had nearly reached the ranch house. Josh stood, the blanket still wrapped around his shoulders. What should he do?

Keeping quiet would give him the advantage over the approaching newcomers. But should he alert the others? Should he shout out a warning?

CHAPTER SIXTY-THREE

"We're here now!" Bill's voice reached Josh's ears. As the buggy drew up to the porch, the slight shaft of moonlight between the clouds lit up the couple sitting on the buggy seat.

Josh felt his shoulders drop, the tension easing out of his body as he walked over to the hitching rail and took the reins from Bill.

"What are you all doing here? It's the middle of the night. How did you manage to travel with so little moonlight?" Josh's questions were ignored.

Bill had jumped down from the buggy, and was reaching up to the dark shape that had been sitting beside him. He took the bundle that she had been clutching from her as Hannah jumped down to join him. To Josh's further surprise, from the back of the buggy a tiny figure slowly rose and climbed down to join the other two.

By this time, the occupants of Broken Horseshoe Ranch had been woken up by the unexpected bustle and noise. They rushed out onto the porch with Amy, who had lit the oil lamp—coming last, but illuminating the scene.

To their amazement, Bill had appeared with baby David in his one arm. Hannah tiptoed onto the porch anxiously, with her arm round Flora. Both Hannah and Flora looked nervous as they gazed round at the figures clustered on the porch, staring at them.

"Am, Am," was followed by a large wail from David.

"Here Amy, take him and give us all peace!" Bill said and pushed the sobbing bundle that was David into Amy's arms.

Josh hurriedly took the oil lamp from her as she held David and murmured soothingly to him. The baby opened his eyes and stared fixedly into Amy's face. It was almost as if he didn't believe she was there. Then, with a great sob, he flung himself into her arms and promptly fell asleep.

The chaos finally subsided as everyone found a spot in which to spend the last few hours remaining of the night. In the morning, everyone was tired and bleary-eyed— except for David. He chuckled and laughed at the people around him, and was crawling everywhere he could. Flora sat quietly in a corner of Amy's bedroom, wide-eyed and amazed at the novelty of the people and scenes around her.

Catching sight of the shy young Apache girl, Amy called to her: "Flora, can you look after David for me? I need to get ready to go out with the others this morning." There was no need to ask Flora twice. In seconds she had joined David on the floor and was carefully guiding him away from the hot stove and anything else that would cause him harm.

"David won't sleep at night without Amy. He's all right during the day. He's used to her going to the general store in Nowhere or out treasure hunting with Josh. But nighttime is when he looks for Amy," Hannah stated, standing at the table. Her hands were anxiously twisting. It had been an ordeal for her coming into the ranch, meeting all these people in the middle of the night. The hugs she received from Amy and Nancy had put her at ease almost immediately. Hannah received a warm welcome from Luke, who thanked her and her son for the medicine that had returned him to a better quality of life. Somehow, Josh thought it had been Chan and Tom who had made her feel most comfortable. Their innate Chinese for the older person came out in their attentiveness towards her.

Luke spoke to Nancy. "We can't leave Nat and Hannah alone at Dry Creek Ranch. There is too much for them to do, and they need constant surveillance and help in case of attack by Jeremiah." Luke sat at the table, his concern evident in the way he kept looking at Nancy. It had been her ranch, and although she spent most of her time at Broken Horseshoe Ranch, he knew how much it meant to her.

Nancy decided she must sort the problem out. Luke's comment and glance towards her had made that plain. "Josh and Amy, you and Ben and Chan go on the treasure hunt as was planned last night. David must stay here. We all need our sleep and, as he will only sleep near to Amy at night, that's settled. I suggest I go back with Bill—and Ezra, if he's willing to go with me back to Dry Creek Ranch. That gives Nat and Bill two others to help in the garden and keep watch."

"But where should I go?" Hannah's faint voice came as she stood nervously in the corner.

"Hannah, you stay here with Flora. You can look after David with Leah and Flora. Tom and Luke are handy with their guns and I know you are too, Hannah. That will mean both ranches have enough people for the moment, until Sam and Matthew return."

There was a bustle at the porch as the buggy was readied for Dry Creek Ranch, and the horses loaded for their trip to the foothills of Devil's Mountain. Amy, before she left, was conscious of the tall woman standing nervously in the corner. Amy knew Hannah was uncertain and afraid of this new experience. Hannah had finally relaxed and settled into Dry Creek Ranch. This was one other new experience she was struggling with.

"Hannah, I know you're going to be looking after

David and Flora." Amy joined Hannah and placed her hand on her arm, whispering to her: "But please, can I ask you to look after my father? He is so much better, but he is constantly overdoing it. Try to make him rest or at least sit down for a while. He gets so tired and it depresses him. I'll be back tonight late. Try to enjoy your time here." Amy leant forward, kissed the older woman on the cheek and ran out of the ranch house across the porch to her waiting horse and the others. The search for the Jesuit treasure was on again.

Amy turned back as they rode off and felt relieved when she saw Hannah standing beside her father. Hannah was taking up duties with Luke immediately. Her gentle father would be good for the woman, and the novelty of Broken Horseshoe Ranch would be a fresh experience for her and Flora.

They rode on for some time, and Josh was amazed at how happy he felt riding out towards Devil's Mountain. He looked at Amy riding alongside him and grinned at her. He could tell by her expression that she too was revelling in the open space and the excitement of seeking further Jesuit treasure. It had been some time since the two of them had done this. Riding into the sunrise was a magical experience. The fingers of light gradually sweeping down the mountain towards the foothills gave them an illuminated pathway on which they could ride. "Over there, near to that rocky ridge. There seem to be small caves in the rock. Then the land sweeps down to a small creek. I think it's always full of water, much like the one at Broken Horseshoe. It doesn't look as if it ever dries up," Ben called out to them and pointed, then rode on ahead of them.

Amy had halted, her eyes sweeping around the land.

She focused her gaze on Devil's Mountain, then on the sharp cliffs of the ridge ahead.

"What is it, Amy?" Josh, noticing her increased interest, rode over to join her. He remembered Amy had been searching for Jesuit gold long before she had found him. He'd been unconscious in the desert, when she had come across him and somehow, despite the lack of water, she had got them both back to the ranch. Since that day, his memory had never returned but he'd become part of the group that made up the makeshift family that lived on Broken Horseshoe Ranch.

"Amy? What have you seen?" Josh's voice was full of excitement. He recognized that look on Amy's face. Her sharp eyes and knowledge of Jesuit treasure signs had borne fruit for them before now. "Amy? What is it?"

CHAPTER SIXTY-FOUR

"Look at that tree! It's old, and very tall, and the top has been cut off." Amy pointed at the tree growing alongside the river. "That used to be a sign that gold was nearby. One of Pa's books tells that the Mormons, when mining for gold, used that—among other signs—to show where they had been digging for gold."

Despite himself, Josh felt the stirring of excitement deep within him. He had told himself so many times not to raise his hopes. Maybe this time would be the lucky time. Surely, there had to be some time that they would actually find the gold. They rode on after the two boys, who had ridden on ahead, eager to reach yesterday's digging. The boys approached the lower slopes beneath a huge outcropping of rock. Both boys dismounted beneath an overhang and tethered their horses to a small copse of trees.

"Look, Amy, we found this rock with the symbol of the cross marked on it. It must be ancient, because it has mossy stuff growing on it." Ben led his sister over to the rock with a carving on it, pointing it out proudly.

Amy nodded agreement, smiled at Ben, and patted him on the back. "Well done, Ben. You found a symbol. It must mean something as it's so old, possibly of the Jesuit times, and has been carved here with a purpose." She wandered along the uneven ground beneath the overhang.

Josh stood back, shielding the sun from his eyes as he looked carefully about him. Hopeful of finding a cave, or a sign of workings of an old mine, he looked along the higher ridges of the rocky overhang. Ben and Chan were searching the ground near the carving, while Amy followed the line of the overhanging rock itself.

Josh walked down to the river. It tumbled over the rocks in a small waterfall: not big, but Josh reckoned in full spate after heavy rain, it would be a powerful sight. As he looked around, he saw small piles of earth alongside the river. They were old, with weeds and grass growing through them.

"There's been activity here. I think someone's been searching for gold along the creek. These piles look as if someone has been panning for gold alongside the water's edge. It might be worth giving it a try, just to see if there is any gold here," Josh said. He went back up to their horses. Ben had packed the dented metal panning dish that Josh had brought back to the ranch after his fight with the miners. Taking it back with him down to the creek, along with a small shovel, he began digging, and placed some of the gravelly soil aside, ready to pan. Ezra had shown him what to do on one of their expeditions into the canyons of Devil's Mountain. Josh never expected to be panning for gold on Broken Horseshoe Ranch land.

"Look, I think there's been a cave over here. It could be an old mine opening!" Amy called to them. She was further along at the bottom of the cliff and was pointing to the darker dirt strewn beneath the overhang. Josh put his pan down and, after promising himself a speedy return to his sorted piles of dirt, walked up to Amy. Ben and Chan had already joined her.

"There is different coloured dirt here. It's all black and stretches down from that small hole. Can you see it? I think this is charcoal from many fires. It's been weathered over the years with rain and wind and is just dark dirt now. Why don't we dig near to that small opening? We must take care checking all the time, in case there are booby traps." Amy looked at the boys and warned them. "Don't get too excited. It might be a false alarm."

Both boys raced back to the horses to get spades and Amy looked at Josh. "What do you think?"

Josh looked along the overhang, noted the dirt and charcoal mixed in with the soil, and the small opening above it, and nodded. "It's a possibility. There's the sign of the tree and the rock, and the mark Luke found on his map. We have followed weaker clues than that," Josh said. "But if you don't need me here, I'll carry on down by the river."

After a few hours, they stopped for lunch, seated beside the river and in the shade of a scraggly tree. The three working at the cave entrance were dirty, with dark dust clinging to their sweaty clothes and limbs. Josh was the only clean one, but he was stiff from the constant digging. Not one of them had found a thing. There seemed to be so much effort put into that morning's work, with so little reward.

Meg, who had been lying beside them, rose to her feet and began growling. Each one of them reached for a weapon. Amy and Josh stood up, each clutching a rifle.

"It's them! Those two men—they're back again!" Ben exclaimed, hand on his pistol.

Josh held his rifle so that the men could see it. He wasn't threatening them: just showing them he was ready for action.

CHAPTER SIXTY-FIVE

They could see the men talking to each other. One seemed to shake his head, and they both turned and rode off.

"They were looking for us. I think having Josh and Amy here frightened them away," Chan said. "Do you think they meant to kidnap *us*, as well as those other boys?" He looked at Josh with a worried expression on his face.

"They came over that hill with a definite purpose in mind. You could tell they were coming down here. But there were too many of us to tangle with, and they could see we were definitely on the alert," Josh said. He stood staring at where the men had been. "What are they doing? Why are they taking young men and boys?"

None of them felt like continuing. It was still afternoon, and they had planned to stay longer. However, the arrival of the men had been disconcerting, and they all felt that there was a possibility that they may return with other men. Packing up was done at speed.

Josh cast a longing look at his workings at the creek bed. There had been only time to pan a little of the stony dirt. It had been without gold, but he felt it was still promising. Tomorrow, they would return tomorrow. Maybe he'd strike it lucky then.

But Josh did not return the following day. It was Josh and Amy's turn to go into the general store. Manuel needed Josh to help with the deliveries. Since the arrival of Jeremiah, so many more of the outlying ranches and homesteads asked Manuel to deliver. No one wanted to encounter the arrogant, bullying man who professed to be working for God. Staying at home and letting Manuel deliver to them meant they could keep out of Jeremiah's way.

The boxes, canvas sacks, and vegetables and fruit had been piled into the wagon, ready and sorted for each ranch and homestead. Manuel and Josh set off, leaving Eliza—with the help of Dora and Amy—to manage the general store and the hardware area.

The chime of the store's bell, hung over the door, announced the arrival of new customers. All eyes turned towards the door as Caleb, the loud-mouthed son of the self-proclaimed prophet Jeremiah, swaggered in, his stepmother Clara timidly trailing behind him. Caleb had a reputation for being a brash, arrogant young man who used his father's influence as if it were a weapon.

"Got some goods here for me. Father said you'd have them ready," he said as he strode up to Eliza, who was standing behind the counter.

"Can I have the payment for them?" Eliza said.

"My father speaks for God. We don't pay for any goods," the young man said and thumped the counter in anger.

Clara stepped forward. She placed a hand on his arm, trying to defuse the situation. "Caleb, please. Just pay for them."

With a speed that surprised everyone, Caleb's hand shot out, striking Clara with a brutal backhanded slap. She staggered back, clutching her bleeding nose, a look of shock and pain on her face.

Eliza rushed forward to help the fallen woman. "You vile creature!" she shouted at the young man as she rushed past him.

Before she could reach Clara, Caleb shoved Eliza with such force she tumbled to the ground, knocking over a display of canned goods.

Amidst the chaos, Caleb's attention became fixed on Amy, who stood beside the door. Grabbing her violently by the arm, he snarled, "You're coming with me, girl."

Meanwhile, Dora, witnessing the unfolding drama, knew she had to act fast. Without hesitation, she retrieved a shotgun from beneath the counter and aimed it at Caleb. "Let the girl go," she said through gritted teeth, her voice trembling with rage.

Caleb laughed, a cruel, mocking sound. "You wouldn't dare."

As his attention was turned towards Dora, Amy pulled her hidden knife from its sheath in her pocket and slashed it across Caleb's face. He howled with pain, releasing his grip on her as blood spurted from the gash.

Furious and humiliated, he staggered back, clutching his bleeding face. "You will pay for this!" he spat, his eyes burning with hatred. "Both of you!"

He stomped out of the door, leaving behind him a silent store with only the sobbing of Clara breaking the silence. Outside, Devil's Mountain stood mute witnesses to the violence that had unfolded within the store.

CHAPTER SIXTY-SIX

This Sunday morning was different from any other Sunday morning Josh remembered at Broken Horseshoe Ranch. This Sunday, there was a feeling of apprehension that events of the day would prove vitally important for the lives of those living in and around the township of Nowhere.

People were talking about the upcoming confrontation between Jeremiah and Lance Grey, who was both a preacher and sheriff. Every Sunday in the saloon, a morning service took place. The drunks from the previous Saturday night were left sitting where they had slept all night. Townspeople arrived, with the women making sure they were accompanied by other women or male family members, all eager to hear Lance Grey's sermon.

They had become used to the man standing up tall and dressed in his familiar black clothes, leading the hymns, and giving them a sermon that appealed to each one of them. The preacher in Lance Grey had a knack for producing quotes from the Bible and discussing them with regard to their daily lives. They understood the parable of the Sower, as most of them worked on the land. The life of Jesus the carpenter was understood by those working with metal and wood, such as the blacksmith and those building the houses and barns. Lance Grey's glass, full at the beginning of the sermon, was topped up a couple of times during his speech. No one minded. This was frontier country. One made do with what one had.

This Sunday was special, and the saloon was crowded. Eliza and Manuel had opened the general store early. They always opened it on Sundays, since they were Catholic and there was no Catholic church near, and they didn't go to the sermons at the saloon. People who came from far away for Sunday service were happy to stock up on supplies and thankful that Manuel had opened the store.

Josh, Amy, Nancy, and Ezra had all made the journey to listen to the sermon from preacher Lance Grey, but also to stand beside him if Jeremiah came in and caused trouble. His threat had been widely broadcast throughout the countryside, and the increased traffic into the town showed the interest this had awoken in the community.

The buggy, and a couple of horses they had ridden in on, were stabled at the back of the general store. Josh walked across the yard to the front of the general store. He stood for a moment watching the arrival of the many buggies and horses as the eager crowd hitched them to rails along Main Street. The early morning sunshine had given way to dark clouds looming over the Devil's Mountain range. Josh stared at it. The sky was getting darker as the clouds gathered into huge banks speeding over the mountains towards Nowhere. He noticed faint lightning and distant thunder over Devil's Mountain.

Ezra joined him; he too was staring into the distance. With his hand shielding his eyes from the sun, the old man shook his head. "Don't like the look of the weather. Sometimes these storms can be pretty fierce."

"The atmosphere has changed. It feels heavy, somehow ominous. I don't like the look of this weather either, Ezra. I don't remember thunderstorms in my past life, just the one we had the other month," Josh said, raging internally at his lack of memory. Why couldn't he remember? He began thinking, but Ezra interrupted those useless thoughts.

"That was a small storm. I'm afraid those clouds look

as if it's going to be a violent, heavy one. Only hope the trail isn't washed out on the way back to Broken Horseshoe Ranch," Ezra said and led the way into the saloon.

Amy went in to the store and told Manuel and Eliza they had arrived and promised she and Josh would come to help out after the service. Manuel always had a big rush of people when the service ended.

Eliza walked over to look out of the window at the crowds of people entering the saloon. "What do you think is going to happen? That Jeremiah and his son Caleb are crazy enough to cause trouble. Look how that Caleb acted yesterday," Eliza said.

"I wish I'd been here. He wouldn't have behaved like that if either Josh or I were here. Reckon he's a bully when there are only females about. But you sure gave him something to think about, Amy. I hear his face was a mess," laughed Manuel.

Amy changed the subject. She didn't like violence and hated having to resort to it. But she'd had no option. Caleb would have dragged her out of the store, and she shuddered to think of what he had intended for her. "What about Clara? Has she gone back to Jeremiah? She is so thin, and looks as if she's been ill treated by them," asked Amy.

"Clara's not going back to them. Clara is staying upstairs. Dora has taken her in and insists that Clara stays with her," Eliza told Amy.

"That's good. I was worried about what would happen to her. Dora will make sure she's all right," Amy replied. "But I'd better go. Nancy is saving me a seat. She's gone into the saloon with Ezra and Josh. But we'll come over after the service to help you out."

When Amy swung open the saloon doors, she discovered a packed crowd inside. There were no seats left that she could see. Familiar faces mingled with those of complete strangers to her, as they stood around talking in groups. She walked further into the saloon and caught sight of Nancy waving to her. Nancy had found a table halfway to the front and set to the side wall. Amy smiled to herself. Nancy would often seek a secluded spot, away from any potential fighting, but still within reach of a nearby exit. Amy joined her party, squeezing amongst those clustered around tables. Avoiding Seth, who was serving drinks as fast as he could, she smiled at the saloonkeeper. He gave her a flustered nod of his head, dumping the drinks down at one table, whilst taking the order from another.

"Seth will have plenty of accounts for you the next time you do them," Nancy said to Amy, as they both watched the saloon keeper rushing around. "There are many people here who never come into town, but everyone has come in to see what's going to happen when Jeremiah arrives."

Silence fell as Lance Grey came to the front of the saloon. He leant against the bar, thanking Seth who pushed a large glass of whiskey towards him. Lance acknowledged the glass of whiskey and raised it to the crowd, watching him. "Never knew my sermons were so powerful that you've all had to squeeze in to hear them today!" He drank from the dark brown liquid, acknowledging the laughter that greeted this remark.

The doors of the saloon burst open with a bang, revealing the tall, imposing figure silhouetted against the sunlight: Jeremiah, with his flowing beard and piercing eyes, carried an air of authority that demanded attention.

Whispers spread like wildfire around the saloon as everyone recognized him. They all knew him. He'd been making his presence felt in the homesteads and ranches around as he preached his gospel of fear, demanding tithes under the threat of divine retribution.

Jeremiah strode in, his voice booming: "Lance Grey! You are a false preacher! You are leading people astray with your watered-down gospel!"

CHAPTER SIXTY-SEVEN

Lance took another sip of his drink and placed the glass down on the counter. He faced the man shouting at the entrance of the saloon. "Jeremiah," he began, speaking calmly. "We are all here in search of salvation. What brings you to our town and into this saloon?"

Jeremiah's face contorted with anger. "*Salvation?* This town needs saving from the likes of you, 'preacher' Lance Grey!" After shouting these angry remarks at Lance, Jeremiah turned to look at the congregation seated around the tables and standing against the walls. "You people have strayed from the path of true salvation. I warn you that the Lord's wrath will be upon you!" As he spoke, a loud clap of thunder could be heard as the storm approached Nowhere.

Murmurs of unease rippled through the crowd. Many had heard of Jeremiah's fanaticism but witnessing it at first hand was another matter. Jeremiah continued shouting at them, his words becoming rambling. With his angry stomping up and down, in the confined space at the back of the saloon, the words lost their power. He remained oblivious to the growing numbers of hushed whispers around him. The townsfolk listening to him remembered how their buildings had been set ablaze. Livestock were slaughtered and walls were defaced with the word 'repent', leading them to understand that Jeremiah's words had provoked someone to carry out these acts of terror.

Lance had let Jeremiah ramble on, realizing that the false prophet's words were no longer as powerful as before. The sheriff-cum-preacher walked forward and raised his hand for silence. The murmurs in the crowd were stilled, and Jeremiah himself stopped talking and looked at Lance in surprise.

Raising a hand towards Jeremiah, Lance said, loudly and with slow deliberation: "Jeremiah, we are a community in Nowhere that has been built through hardship, with faith and trust in each other and in the Lord. If you wish to preach in Nowhere, do so with love and not with threats."

There were murmurs of assent, and some folk shouted *amen* to Lance's words. He continued speaking: "Demanding money from the poor, hardworking folk of this town and the outlying area, with threats of death and destruction, are not the words and deeds of a God-fearing man. I will share with you the words of the prophet Jeremiah from the Bible. It says, 'For I know the plans I have for you', declares the Lord, 'plans to prosper you and not to harm you, plans to give you hope and a future.' Those are the words of the true Jeremiah, the man of God. Look for yourselves in Jeremiah 29:11."

Lance pointed a finger at the man standing in the saloon's doorway. "You are a man of evil and shall perish because of your own sins." Thunder boomed with an earthshaking noise, and a flash of lightning lit up the increasing darkness of the saloon.

Jeremiah stood silent, staring at Lance Grey. The people in the saloon looked around at each other, nodded their heads, and looked at their resident preacher with a dawning respect.

Lance spoke again: "Jeremiah, you threatened retribution on these poor folks if they didn't pay you or pray with you. I fear that the retribution you threatened will be on your head, not theirs."

The chatter of voices grew in the saloon as each turned

to their neighbours to discuss this latest turn of events. The words of Lance Grey and those from the Bible seemed to echo around the saloon and were repeated from one person to the other.

"Do you think he's done it? Will Jeremiah leave? Has Lance Grey said enough to influence people and turn them away from Jeremiah?" Nancy asked the others seated at the table beside her.

"I don't know," Josh said. "Jeremiah is just standing there. He has gone red in the face and he's clenching his fists. Shush—he's going to speak."

The crowd of people who were conversing excitedly gradually grew aware that Jeremiah was about to speak, and the noise subsided. A silence fell over the whole of the saloon. No one moved; no one drank from their glasses. All eyes were on Jeremiah at first, then swivelled back to look at Lance Grey.

Drinking his whiskey, Lance's casual manner hid the inner turmoil of the man. Josh could see it in the nervous tic at his jawline, and his hand clenching and unclenching.

Jeremiah shouted into the uneasy silence: "You quote the Bible at me, but you stand here drinking, in a den of iniquity, with sinners and drunkards. I tell all of you present: unless you get up and follow me out of the saloon now and fall on your knees to pray outside on Main Street, you *will* be damned!" He raised both arms up to heaven and screamed at them. "Outside and pray! Or you will be damned!" Thunder echoed around Nowhere; lightning flashed again.

Silence fell in the saloon. No one moved, and it was in that uneasy quiet that a voice could be heard outside: "Repent! The end is nigh! The time for the end of the world has come upon us. Repent!"

CHAPTER SIXTY-EIGHT

The harsh voice shouting outside grew louder. Other voices could be heard, also shouting, and women had begun screaming. The storm that had been threatening the entire day had reached Nowhere. The black clouds that had been looming over Devil's Mountain, threatening rain, now descended in full force over the township.

A thunderclap reverberated throughout the saloon and the town itself. The very ground seemed to shake as the echo of the thunder drifted up to the mountains. Lightning flashed again and again, its brilliant glare illuminating the saloon.

Outside, the yelling continued. Over all the shouts and screams, a voice rose in volume, shouting again and again: "Repent! Retribution is upon the town. Repent!"

The saloon emptied as each person pushed past the other to see what was happening. Everyone rushed out through the swing doors. There was a constant pushing and shoving. No one wished to be left behind.

Lance Grey stalked up to the swing doors. Jeremiah had been out first. The others were now crowding around him outside on Main Street. Josh and Amy followed Nancy and Ezra, who had been eager to join the first ones out of the saloon. They stood back, allowing Lance to proceed before them.

Josh stood with Amy on the boardwalk of the saloon, staring in horror at the sight. Nowhere was on fire! Flames were leaping up vigorously from the livery stable. Horses were squealing in fright, but Reuben the blacksmith was already leading them to safety. Other horses, tethered around Main Street, were anxious in the face of the storm. People were screaming, whilst others were dashing up and down to put out the fires.

"It's Caleb! Josh, he has a torch, and he's going to set fire to the general store! We must stop him!" cried Amy. They both ran across Main Street, determined to stop him before he could set the general store building alight.

But there was no need for them to run. Manuel and Dora both stood, one with a shotgun and the other had a pistol pointed at Caleb. Manuel walked to the end of the boardwalk: "Don't come any nearer. Throw that torch down. You'll not set my store alight and live." His voice bellowed, the pistol pointing straight at Caleb's head. Manuel's other hand was hitching up his voluminous canvas trousers. Despite the horror of the moment, Josh had to hide a smile at the sight. The capacious trousers always had trouble with Manuels's enormous belly.

Main Street was full of people rushing about, screaming and shouting. Jeremiah stood transfixed. For once, he was speechless. He could only stare his at his son in horror and disbelief.

Lance Grey stood for a moment, assessing the situation, looking up and down Main Street. Then he acted. His voice rang out the length of the Main Street: "Reuben, settle all the horses! Seth, you and the other men get buckets in a line, and put out those fires before they take hold!"

Thunder boomed again, and the dark clouds were menacingly hanging directly over the town, turning it into a dark pit with fires burning on each side. Nancy drew closer to Amy. She linked arms with her. "It's as if the Devil himself has come to visit Nowhere," she whispered to the girl.

Amy nodded, but she was intent on Caleb. She had seen Lance look at him, but his attention had been turned away from Caleb as he concentrated on the fires. Nowhere was a fledgling town, mostly constructed of timber and, in some cases, canvas tents. Dangerously inflammable, it wouldn't have taken much to destroy the entire town.

Wind whipped the smoke from the fires, sparks fluttering about in whirlwinds of dangerous flying embers. Everyone was in fear of the fire, knowing how it could leap from building to building with the wind. Another lightning flash was accompanied by a thunderclap so deafening that it shook the very ground. Then it came. Rain fell from the sky in torrential gusts, sweeping down the street, lashing faces, and bodies. No one complained. No one objected to the downpour that was flooding the very street itself.

"The rain is putting out the fires. Thank *God*— He has sent the rain," Nancy said, her hands clenched as if in prayer.

Amy was still looking at Caleb. She could see the angry red wound across his face. Her knife had left its mark.

Still, he was marching up and down, waving a burning torch, his voice shrill with venom and hatred: "Repent! The end is nigh!" The rage that had been directed at the women in the general store was now directed at the whole town. He was venting his fury on them and was determined to make them pay for not obeying him or his father. The last flurry of the downpour of rain extinguished the fire in his torch. Now, he was waving a smoking brand in the air.

All the while, Jeremiah had stood with his eyes wide with horror at the devastation that his son had caused. He didn't move, unable to believe that his son could have caused the burnings, animal deaths, and had painted the word 'repent' everywhere.

Then he acted. Even amidst the fire, rain, and panic, Jeremiah's shouts could be heard. He bellowed, his words cutting across the noise: "Caleb? What have you done?"

CHAPTER SIXTY-NINE

Jeremiah's voice was heard by his son, who was halfway up Main Street. Caleb abruptly halted and turned, staring directly at his father. He retraced his steps back towards the saloon. The panicked townspeople were still rushing around frantically, trying to douse the flames and salvage what they could. Amidst the chaos, father, and son walked towards each other.

Amy grabbed Josh's arm and watched the scene unfold before her. Nancy, who was standing beside the couple, took a deep breath before whispering, "What's going to happen now? Caleb looks as if he has gone mad. It's obvious now—just as we thought—he was behind all the things his father predicted. It was Caleb who burned down the buildings, killed the animals, and painted the threats over the walls."

"Jeremiah didn't know it was his son. Did he?" Amy asked the others. "Could he really have been ignorant of what his son was doing?"

Josh shook his head. "Do you know, I honestly think Jeremiah didn't realize his son was behind everything. Jeremiah must have really believed that he had the power to cause all the havoc and mayhem that ensued after his damnation predictions."

Caleb, by this time, had almost reached his father. His face became contorted with madness as he faced Jeremiah, a twisted smile playing on his lips. "I'm just doing God's work, Father. Isn't this what you have preached? I'm doing the work for you and God."

Even in the thunderstorm's gloom, Josh could see Jeremiah's face grow pale. The enormity of his son's actions was finally becoming apparent and was weighing heavily on the man. Jeremiah finally spoke to his son. "This isn't the way. God would have done what I asked of him."

Caleb sneered at that remark. He took yet another step nearer to his father: "*I* did what you asked—*not* God! Don't you understand? It was I who carried out your predictions of retribution. I am the power of retribution, not you!" Caleb shrieked the words to his father.

Finally, the fires—with the help of the rainstorm—had been put out. The damage had been minimal. Caleb had been discovered before the fires took hold. The townspeople began to notice the drama now being acted out on Main Street. They stood silently, up and down the street. Some were dirty with smoke and had empty buckets in their hands. Others stood with the horses. Yet still more had dropped everything to come forward. As one, they realized that their ordeal and torment had not come from God. Caleb had been the instrument of their hardship. He had been the one carrying out Jeremiah's predictions.

"It seems impossible that Jeremiah didn't realize what Caleb was doing. Surely, he must have thought it strange that everything happened after he'd predicted it?" Nancy said.

Josh replied, "Jeremiah thought he was a prophet. He deluded himself into thinking he had power. And his delusion has wrought havoc on the mind of his son."

The rain had stopped. The wind dropped, leaving behind an eerie silence. Water dripped off roofs and ran down porches to splash into the growing puddles. Feet coming closer to see the argument between father and son could be heard as they splashed through the pools of water left by the torrential downpour.

But, still in the background, the rumble of thunder was hovering over Devil's Mountain. Lightning still flashed, illuminating the dramatic scene being played out in front of everyone on the main street of Nowhere.

Jeremiah rushed towards his son. He put out a hand towards him in a gesture of reconciliation. "This is all wrong. This is evil. You are not carrying out the Lord's work. You have been an instrument of the Devil himself!" The brutal words fell into the silence. The townsfolk of Nowhere were watching and listening, open-mouthed. So many had suffered at the hands of these two, had lived in fear of Jeremiah's evil predictions. No one was going to miss a single word either of them said.

All eyes now turned to Caleb. His face was contorted with a vicious anger directed towards his father.

Amy clutched Josh's arm tighter this time. "What will Caleb do now?"

CHAPTER SEVENTY

Caleb stood facing his father. His father's pleading was ignored. Caleb seemed to come to a realization of his surroundings and the people who stood in groups watching him. The looks of horror and anger from the crowd made his face distort into a demonic smile. Caleb touched the raw red gash on his face on his face; he winced at the pain of it.

Amy saw this, and she felt delighted at his suffering. The callous brutality of his blow on Clara's face had been done with no mercy on his part. He hadn't cared that he was inflicting suffering on a frail woman. Amy could only watch and hope no one else suffered at the hands of Caleb.

Jeremiah stood, the look of despair growing on his face as he looked at his son. "Caleb, this is not the Lord's work you are doing: you terrorized these people, you destroyed their property. How could you think that was doing good?" Again, Jeremiah held out his hand towards his son.

The storm, which had drifted away, seemed to circle back to Nowhere. The torrential showers had flooded Main Street but, to the relief of the inhabitants of the town, it had quenched the fires that Caleb had started.

Thunder boomed overhead and lightning flashed, as if the storm hadn't quite finished with the townsfolk of Nowhere. Several people looked up at the sky, and Josh could see their lips moving as if in prayer. He even caught sight of a few people crossing themselves in the manner of the Catholics. Josh knew they weren't Catholics. But in the heat and fury of the storm, and the emotional fear that had been wrought within the people, anything to relieve the tension was welcome.

"Caleb, this isn't the way. That wasn't God's work." Jeremiah had almost reached his son.

Caleb's face grew dark with anger. "Maybe it's not the way you wanted but, Father, this is my way!" So, saying these words, Caleb threw the smoking torch on the ground. It landed in a puddle, giving a weak sizzle as it finally died.

Josh felt Amy move closer towards him. He looked down at her, at her expression. It's almost as if she knew what was coming but was powerless to stop it, he thought.

"This is my way, Father!" The gunshot rang out and Jeremiah crumpled to the ground, a look of shock etched upon his face. Caleb's movement had been swift, and no one could have guessed that he would have acted in such a way.

His loud laughter rang out. The townsfolk could only stare in appalled horror. No one moved. That unexpected shot, felling Jeremiah to the ground, had caused consternation.

"My way!" Caleb looked down at the dead body of his father. "My way, Father!" Another shot rang out, and the body of Caleb sprawled beside his father amongst the puddles and the falling rain on the main street of Nowhere.

The rain stopped. Thunderclouds black and heavy, moved away over the Devil's Mountains. Whispering townsfolk approached the two bodies, their dismay and shock apparent in the hushed voices and solemn faces. Nowhere' s street was flooded with puddles, and the charred buildings remained standing in defiance of Caleb's wicked deeds. Suddenly, they were bathed in sunlight.

The sun's rays caused the ground to steam, and the wisps wreathed the air as the sudden heat enveloped the town.

Lance Grey's voice rang out as he strode to the middle of the street to address the people: "Tragedies came to our town today. Jeremiah often preached about retribution. Today, he himself felt to the full what retribution meant. People, go on about your normal Sunday business. We will bury these two, but the terror and fear that they brought to the townsfolk of Nowhere is over. Let's enjoy the sunshine of the day and mop up after the storm." He turned away from the folk who were still standing around the bodies. They were excitedly discussing the events of the morning—indeed over the past few weeks, since the arrival of Jeremiah and his family.

"Seth," Lance Grey called out. "Seth, I need a large whiskey. Now!"

Nancy put one arm through Ezra's and another through Josh's, and spoke to them both. Her glance included Amy as she said, "That *is* a good idea! How about we go in and join the preacher?"

Amy shook her head. "I'll go over to help in the general store. I promised Manuel and Eliza, and I reckon they will be busy once this crowd finishes talking over the morning's events. You stay for a while, Josh. You can join me later."

CHAPTER SEVENTY-ONE

The place was bustling with activity. So many people came into the general store to buy provisions after the drama with Jeremiah. Their purchases made, they chatted with one another so that the store was full of people. Manuel was irritable and would have loved to hurry them out, but knew that wasn't the right thing to do if he wished to keep their goodwill.

After the crowd slowly drifted away, and all those who had come in to see the Jeremiah showdown had left for home, Manuel thanked Amy: "It made all the difference having you here this morning. We have been so busy and have sold most of the fruit and vegetables. Please see if you can get some more from Nancy and bring it in tomorrow."

Amy was about to answer Manuel, but she heard the voice call her name. She gave Manuel a nod and turned round.

"Miss Amy—I've heard it was you who gave Caleb that vicious wound across his face. I'm amazed that such a gentle lady like yourself could do that," Charles Roberts's voice came from behind her.

Before Amy could answer him—because she didn't really know what to say—Dora stepped forward.

"Any woman would have done that if she was grabbed by the arm and dragged towards the door. It didn't matter whether or not she was a gentle lady. Any woman would fight to protect herself."

Charles smiled at Dora, nodding his head. "There's such a lot of death around the general store. It's quite a nasty situation. Let's hope that's the end for now. Although I wouldn't be too sure that murder is very far away—not with some of the folk you have working here." His last words were meant for Amy to take back to Josh. Of that, Amy was certain. However, those words of his were meaningless to anyone else listening. The man was clever, Amy thought. He would need to be watched carefully if they were hoping to get the better of him.

Josh appeared, with a grizzled old man following behind him. Nancy and Ezra had already returned to the Broken Horseshoe Ranch.

"Are you ready? This is Red. He's going to be joining us at the ranch."

Manuel looked at the old-timer and smiled at him. "What's this, Red? Not going prospecting again? Never thought to see you living on a ranch."

Scratching his bald head, his few remaining white-haired strands showing no sign of the bright red hair he'd had when he was young, the old prospector shook his head ruefully at Manuel. "Broke my leg—healed up all right, but no good for climbing mountains or prospecting around on my own. Things are strange now up in the mountains. Bad men up there, looks like they are grabbing the young ones. Heard tell of yet another young lad disappearing. Think I'm better off with a roof over my head at a ranch."

Manuel nodded agreement. "Never heard you speak so much, Red. Reckon that broken leg of yours has loosened your tongue. They're fine people at Broken Horseshoe Ranch. You'll be all right with them." Manuel patted the old man on the back and turned to Amy. "Red is a good one. Honest and straightforward—glad it's you lot he's going to live with."

As they were about to leave, loaded up with provisions for Tom and Nancy, Eliza came up to them. Before Amy could stop her, she told Josh about the visit of Charles Roberts and how he was warning of yet further deaths to come around the general store. "Didn't like him saying that. Makes me worry. Had enough death and destruction for the time being. Don't want any more." Eliza went off, shaking her head at the very thought of more murders to come.

Josh's eyebrow went up quizzically as he looked at Amy. She nodded, unable to speak with Red and Manuel standing beside them. Nevertheless, Josh realized that Charles Roberts was issuing another warning. And that warning was for him!

Josh and Amy rode off towards Broken Horseshoe Ranch, the old prospector Red beside them. They couldn't talk with him there but both knew what the other was thinking. The danger following Josh, from the man seeking his death, had not gone away. Charles Roberts was warning him yet again. His life was still in danger! Josh vowed to himself that no longer would he sit and wait for the next killer to arrive in Nowhere. No, he would seek not only the killers out, but the man behind them too. Josh promised himself that he would look for this man and find out the reason he wanted him dead!

"Don't like this business of the disappearance of the young men. What's it all about?" Red said as they rode along. The old-timer had a small mule following his horse, with all his worldly possessions on it—mainly prospecting equipment.

"Something has to be done about it, because I'm worried about Tom, Chan, and Ben," Amy said in reply. "Two men have already been looking at them as if they wanted to take them away."

"At least we don't have to worry about Jeremiah any

more. Both ranches don't need to be on such high alert," Josh said.

They rode on in silence, each one of them thinking back to the dramatic scene between Jeremiah and his son, the storm, and their terrible ending.

As they continued to Broken Horseshoe Ranch, Josh's eyes continually strayed to the equipment that was laden on Red's mule. Perhaps, with Red's help, he could find gold. Maybe not Jesuit gold. It would be good to find Josh's gold! He rode on to Broken Horseshoe Ranch with a smile on his face.

About The Author

Janey Clarke writes charming, witty, cosy mysteries. From septuagenarian shenanigans in Cornwall to the intrigue of Regency-era whodunits and now to her newest venture into the rugged drama of the Wild West. When not plotting her next twist or researching historical details, she can be found exploring the stunning Jurassic Coast in Dorset with her loyal spaniel by her side. With a passion for tea, old books, and well-timed humour, Janey Clarke creates stories she hopes will whisk readers away to delightful worlds where solving a mystery is always the order of the day. And always solved by a feisty heroine! Visit Janey at www.janeyclarke.com to learn more about her books.

www.blossomspringpublishing.com

www.ingramcontent.com/pod-product-compliance
Lightning Source LLC
Chambersburg PA
CBHW050725180626
46814CB00002B/600